Dirty Money
and other stories

Also by Ayn Imperato:

Greyhound to Wherever
(Andromeda Press)

Dirty Money
and other stories

Ayn Imperato

Manic D Press
San Francisco

Published by Manic D Press.

Cover design: Scott Idleman/BLINK

A CIP catalog record for this book is available
from the Library of Congress.
ISBN 0-916397-61-0

Distributed by Publishers Group West

for my cowpoke boy

Contents

Mr. Janglin' Bones and the Brain

We should have known it couldn't last. Our little backroom insanity. People can't keep their traps shut and everyone wants a piece of the action. Pretty soon the action's gone.

It all went down at The Crypt, a Gothic store on Haight Street in San Francisco where lots of morbid kids in black and pointy buckle boots would trudge in lamenting about life in the dreary suburbs and then spend what was a week's worth of pay for me on a bunch of rubber eyeballs, bat wall hangings, and cheap Ankh jewelry.

When there was a loud noise in the store this big toy skeleton leftover from Halloween called Mr. Janglin' Bones would start vibrating and cackling over in the corner. During our store meetings when we would all laugh out loud at something, Mr. Janglin' Bones would laugh along with us.

There is no greater source of total mental breakdown then retail employment. Over the course of the year I worked at the store, we got into tons of brawls with Haight Street acid trip casualties who would come in and harass us over one thing or another. Once a young street punk came in babbling about his experience being drawn up into the sky by vampires, then refused to leave the store. He stood by the incense logs for well over an hour, staring into space until he finally shuffled off. One time some guy I had never seen before came in and asked me out. When I said no, he stole my leopard day planner when I wasn't looking and dumped it down the street. Apparently he gleaned my phone number from the book first because he called my house once every hour for days until my boyfriend at the time - tired of being woken up at 4 a.m. - picked up the phone and threatened to rip him in half. Then the calls ceased. Another day a recently let-out sex offender came in and grabbed Maria's breast. All this for five or six bucks an hour. After a while I came to the realization I could be working in a psycho ward dealing with the same people for double the wages.

Sometimes cool stuff happened too. Once a homeless guy came in and gave me a dead spider. An eighteen-year-old street punk came in wearing a ruffley tuxedo shirt and told me in a very distinguished and assumed English accent about his life hustling on Polk Street. Then he was out the door and I never saw him again.

I don't know what kept us all going on. It was a cool store in its own way. Everyone who worked at The Crypt was some sort of misfit — writers, artists, witches, psychics, psychotics, punks, Goth-damaged clubbers. Some of us hung in there for the long haul. Other people came and went. The psychics - Senore and Mick - offered us much-needed daily spiritual advice. Tawnee was a beautiful, funny, always mega-stressed-out, running around like a body without a grave, Goth woman. Jill was my artist partner in crime. Hawk was a sweet, twisted Goth boy with hair that stood out all over in a spray of spikes as if shocked by an electrical source. We sold these squeaking toy nuns which he hated because they made a really annoying sound and when someone would squeak one, Hawk would pop out of nowhere, his ratty hair standing out all over, with this twisted expression on his face. He really hated those squeak nuns. Senore and Jill found out about my deep, deep horror of clowns and mercilessly hid various clown pictures and objects like rubber noses among my personal effects. It was that kind of place.

It never seemed so bad because I was surrounded by people I could relate to in some way. But it wasn't exactly a healthy work environment. The owner, Jewel, would only show up periodically to wreck the relationships between everyone involved with the place. She'd start the gossip flow by whispering one thing to one person and one thing to another and then flit off to Europe to "de-stress" leaving us to undo the damage. She also liked to play musical managers appointing one person in charge one week and another person in charge the next, leaving everyone with their own chaotic reality.

Well, when she wasn't around things went great. Me and Hawk were left to manage the store for a time without much instruction other then to "keep things running" which we did surprisingly efficiently. Except for one big flub up. That's when it all went down.

Well, one day one of our regular customers came in with a strange bundle wrapped up in a beige rag and whispered, "Hey, do you guys want to buy a human brain?" He pulled the piece of cloth aside. Underneath was a brain floating in a clear cookie jar. We all had a good chuckle over it until we realized that the guy was for real. "I just got it from my cousin in Mexico," he explained

I shook my head. *Oh God. This job.* In fact, it wasn't a totally crazy proposition since we sold animal bones and bugs a-plenty, so what was a human brain in a cookie jar?

At that moment some people walked in so I stepped aside to help them. When I turned around a few minutes later, the guy and his brain were gone.

After everyone had left the store, Hawk came downstairs from the back room. He had this evil grin on his face. He looked around and whispered, "I want to show you something!" I followed him up the stairs and saw the brain sitting on a chair in the back room. I looked at the brain all swelled and wrinkly and pink, engorged with formaldehyde where there once were blood and thoughts. I noticed a slice towards the front like someone had taken this dude out with an axe. This was the stuff cheap horror flicks were made of, only this was real life.

"Oh shit! You took the brain!" I exclaimed. "What, did you lose your head or something?" Ha ha ha. Turns out that unbeknownst to me, Hawk took the guy upstairs and agreed to sell the brain on consignment for him. I looked up to see Hawk swinging a plastic hatchet. "I want to brain thee!" he screamed.

Well, it was all in good fun, but I finally mentioned that it was probably risky to have it in our possession, especially damaged like that and that we better keep it under wraps lest we both get hauled off as accessories to a murder rap for housing body parts.

Of course that didn't last long. After a few days we had everyone we knew parading back there to check out the sideshow. Half the employees of Haight Street came in for the spectacle. Goth kids in black came by to pray over the closest thing to actual death they had ever seen. People brought food and drinks. It was the best party in town.

Needless to say, eventually the owner Jewel discovered it and boy did she ever freak. Now she had something real to freak about. She called the coroners and immediately fired Hawk - or should I say wrote his epitaph - after he admitted to the crime. That totally sucked because Hawk was so great to work with and had put so much blood and sweat into the store. But even my testimony in his defense couldn't save him.

Nothing I could have said would have mattered anyway. The bloated brain - floating silently in a clear, barely-taped-shut cookie jar of formaldehyde - pretty much said it all.

After the store closed, the coroners came. They were a real bunch. They had official uniforms on but had big silly grins on when they came inside. You'd think a regular brain-in-a-jar would be old hat for these fellows, but they certainly seemed amused by the situation. One guy picked up the brain and started shaking it around in the jar, watching it's rubbery brain self banging around inside the glass, cackling at the little brain pieces falling around the jar like snow. That's when it started to leak.

It was only taped together by some regular strapping tape but that just busted wide open when the coroner decided to play snow globe with the brain-in-jar. So now there was brain juice dripping down on the floor and I could tell Jewel was perturbed but she was in no position to squabble, what with an unidentified brain in her store.

I asked the coroner, "So what are you going to do with it?"

"I don't know," he answered, "Probably destroy it."

"You're not going to use that jar for cookies later, are you?" I laughed.

His face wrinkled up. "Gross!" he said.

"I can't believe I just grossed out a coroner!"

"You did!" he assured me and I felt very proud because grossing out a man who scoops up dead people all day long was surely an accomplishment.

So when all was said and done, they got ready to leave and we all stood around the stain on the wood floor. One of the guys said, "Next time someone brings you a brain, call us *a-head* of time! Ha ha!"

The coroners, Jewel and I all laughed. Mr. Janglin' Bones cackled along with us from his corner.

Cow Head

Last night I had a dream about a big cut-off cow head I had to prepare for some special event. I had to dress it up and make it look "nice" and arrange its teeth which kept falling out.

Freedom and Rubber Eyeballs

The Crypt's death trip gave me a death wish. Not only was it gloomy as fuck in there, but nothing is more meaningless then retail employment. Underpaid, underappreciated, counting coins, bagging product, "smiles everyone, smiles" - smiles behind gritted teeth. The worst was the boredom. Between the insanity were hours of empty labor. Often left to work alone in the store, sometimes hours would pass without a single person passing through the front door. Days turned to months. My mind into mush. I found myself drowning in monotony. Its tidal wave broke over my back and took me down. I had to get out. But how?

Meanwhile I passed the hollow hours in other ways. I bought a wedge of clay at the art store down the street. Between sales I molded it into weird shapes and prayed for a power outage. After a week or so I had molded a woman on her hands and knees, bound and gagged. I hid it in the back room and there it sat behind a bag of plastic bats like a testament to my fate. A week later the owner rematerialized and I had to crush it back into a blob of clay to destroy the evidence. Days later the store mysteriously closed. It was like my magic wish had been answered. Free. Free. I could get unemployment for a while and have some goddamn time again.

On my last night there I surveyed my sad, useless-product kingdom. I was never fucking coming back. I took my clay blob under my arm and a handful of rubber eyeballs for the road and hit it.

Dirty Money

Mundo sat across from me in the restaurant mutilating his omelette with a fork. I sat staring out the huge bay windows at the early morning street, the people rushing by like they were actually going somewhere real *important*. Not like they were just going to their lame ass jobs.

One day I was working a retail position at a Gothic store that sold gargoyles, capes, magic supplies, and rubber toys on Haight Street. The next day I wasn't. The store shut down suddenly and there I was — BAM— unemployed, sitting in this cafe drinking coffee like it was my new profession wondering how the fuck I was going to make rent at the end of the month.

Half the time I worked at that store I was employed under the table, so it turned out I wasn't eligible for unemployment for at least a month. Now after working my ass off shlepping gargoyle statuettes to Goth-damaged suburbanites for a year in a place where "frequent psychotic episodes" was a reasonable job requirement, I was ready for a break. The fact that my right to unemployment checks were denied had left me pretty grim. Mundo was in a similar position conveniently laid off the same week as me, so now we could kick it and suffer and play and fuck and scrimp our pennies and run around and bitch & moan and celebrate our beautiful unemployment together.

But then reality strikes with his nasty fists. The money factor. Rent was almost due and there were bills to be paid and the food and the coffee- justifiable in rough times as an appetite suppressant and depression annihilator- were all necessary for survival.

I looked over at Mundo. He had cut his biscuit in half and was making it bark like a dog. Was this really our fate?

I scanned the classifieds in the local free papers for hope. I considered the "Ladies needed for nude magazines" ad. "$800 a day." It was tempting, but I decided against it. At least for now. Sure it would be quick cash, but I just wasn't ready to open next week's paper to find my face and leopard-bikini-clad body next to the 976-PUNK ad. Gruesome. I tried other options.

"Look Mundo!" I exclaimed. "Thousands weekly stuffing envelopes. That's how I'm going to make my *millions*."

He looked up at me and grimaced.

"Oh, shut up," I muttered. "*Millions*." I wasn't going to let my dreams be snuffed by a boy who makes his biscuit bark like a dog. Then I stumbled across a viable prospect. "Cash for messy models. Glamor 'mud' shots. Look better in mud."

I thought, okay. I can sploosh around in mud for awhile for some cash. How bad could it be? It didn't sound pornographic. And I mean, what the hell else better did I have to do?

That afternoon I went home and called the number. The photographer was very enthusiastic. "Well," he explained. "What I'm trying to do here is to create a scene with *primal people* coming out of a mud pit, kind of like a Darwin thing. Like fish coming out of the primordial soup. Only with nude, mud-covered humans."

Okay. Whatever. "So I have to take my clothes off?"

"Yes," he said, a little too enthusiastically. "But it's not like that. I assure you it's not pornographic. More *artistic.*"

"Can my boyfriend come and watch?"

"Well, he can if he participates!"

"Cool," I said. "I think he'd be into it. I'll get back to you." I hung up. I sure as hell wasn't going to go to a mud quarry out in the middle of bumfuck San Jose nowhere by myself with a strange man and get nude and submerge myself in goop while he took pictures. That would be stupid.

So I asked Mundo if he needed an extra hundred bucks. "Hell, yeah," he said. Then I told him what it was about. He was reluctant and first, but within ten minutes he was getting all Darwin on me, practicing his new role as primordial beast. He got totally worked up about it. "Let's do it right now! I wanna get down and dirty in da mud!"

The next day I called to set it up and to agree on the terms. A hundred dollars each for the day, plus contact sheets and two 8" x 10" prints from the shoot. Cool. The photographer scheduled a date for us. "Set in mud," as he put it.

The night before the shoot we practiced our "primal moves," the funniest being Mundo mounting me from behind with his best Neanderthal look on, grunting, "Duh!" If nothing else, this would be amusing.

So we drove down to San Jose and met the photographer dude. He was largely as I expected. Upper middle class grey haired dude with wild eyes and a loud shirt and a red four wheeler to take us into the depths of the quarry pit for our nude-mud extravaganza. He was friendly. He gave us the hundred bucks up front, cash, which was cool. After that I relaxed a bit. At least it wasn't a scam. We drove up and down through the mountains and quarries which were really, really gorgeous. He spread blankets down for us in the woods, happily chattering away about this camera filter and that photo shoot and how good the mud felt. He even turned away while we undressed and picked our nude way down the rocks into the mud.

We had to cover every inch in mud- our bodies, face, hair. Everything. We made crusty punks look like Ivory soap girls. We slipped into the slippery mud and spread it on each other's bodies. The photographer held up a mirror and it looked like were wearing slick body stockings. It was incredibly erotic and we laughed and spread the mud around and hugged and kissed our muddy kisses and had a good time.

The photographer came down into the mud with us and started snapping. He let us do pretty much whatever we wanted, yelling "Stop!" or "Hold that! Hold that!" when he wanted a particular shot. We slopped around, acting primal, climbing on top of each other, pretending to rise screaming out of the mud. But after a while we settled down. I tried to keep it classy, moving into a lot of statuesque poses which, luckily, he dug. I'd be damned if I was gonna pose in a muddy pornographic shoot for a hundred measly bucks.

After a while though, he started to get demanding. "What I really want," he said, "is some muddy EROTIC shots." So we got a bit more erotic and I opened up a bit more. He began to shout, "Spread your legs! Get on top of him!"

Okay. Okay. I kept reminding myself that lots of folks in Beverly Hills would pay a bundle at a spa for a mud job like this.

"I wanted to get some shots of a man with an ERECT PENIS covered in mud. Can you work him up a bit?"

So I did my deed but even though Mundo looks so sexy slathered in mud, it was awkward and strange with the dude just standing there. We kept on playing around, touching and kissing and posing with the dude periodically yelling, "Work his penis! Work his penis!" which made us bust up laughing. Sometimes he'd say, "Raise your ASS up in the air. Like that! Yes! Yes!" and snap a shot.

Okay, so this was sort of like soft porn for a hundred bucks. Whatever. The guy was harmless. It was funny. Plus the mud felt really, really luscious. It would have been incredibly relaxing and erotic if the photographer hadn't been there yelling, "Straddle him! Straddle him!"

Anyways, although the mud ended up dying my hair *mud brown*, it was all worth it. I had mud in my ears, in my eyes, in my crotch and a hundred bucks in my pocket. And a boyfriend who would play Neanderthal with me in a pit full of sludge. What more could a strapping girl need?

Dirtier Money

During our unemployment stint, Mundo and I responded to an open call in the local alternative paper for movie extras in the feature film, *What Dreams May Come*, starring Robin Williams and some other big shots. After waiting in line for close to an hour and a half to turn in our photos and bio sheets, we were disappointed when we didn't get a call back. Several months later, however, the casting group called both of us up and asked if we wanted to be "refugees in hell" for the picture. We said, "Yes, of course," as one would be foolish to have her moment as denizen of the underworld pass by.

It was to be shot in Vallejo, California, so we drove on up there on our scheduled date and time. We were bussed onto the set at 4:30 p.m. to find a gigantic pirate ship looming in the distance, a sunken treasure ship made of foam, covered with torn flags and dilapidated boards. Around the ship were bonfires, the dock littered with debris.

I thought, this is kinda cool. We went into wardrobe where our transformation into refugees from hell began and we had to put on these black tattered clothes. When it was my turn to be issued my rags, the woman immediately asked me, "Will you go bare?"

"What?"

"Will you go bare? Kinda risque?"

"Uh, I guess so, " I answered without giving it much thought. She handed me a tiny black worn bustier and a pair of torn black wool leggings. I thought it was a pretty cool outfit until I put it on, walked out of the dressing room, raised my arms and watched as my boobs popped promptly out of the bustier in front of, oh, maybe a hundred people. Whoops.

They gave me another top, kind of like a rag with straps and lace around the top. I strapped it on along with my air-conditioned wool leggings and muddy boots and was on my way.

Before we boarded the next bus, I took a look around at all the girls and guys all busting out of their torn rags. "I give this picture a month at best before it goes to video," I muttered to a fellow refugee.

"Two weeks, tops," she said, pulling at her shredded bra. There was something about scantily clad refugees in hell covered in mud that screamed, "Video!"

We were loaded up into a bus that took us to a giant warehouse where we were to be muddied. Mundo and I pinched ourselves to make sure we weren't in a drug-induced dream. Everywhere we looked there were mud-covered Hell denizens in rags, some wearing little more then thongs and thin strips of cloth across their groins and maybe their breasts. I never saw so many butts in one venue as I did that evening. You wouldn't see that many men's bare rear ends at a festival in the Castro. Everywhere I looked it was butts, butts, butts. The warrior dudes were the most scantily dressed. The warriors had tiny strips of fabric running up their cracks that was little more than butt floss. In contrast to the lowly floss, they had these huge metal warrior breastplates tied across their shoulders and chests and heavy warrior helmets tipped down over their eyes.

Breastplates. Butt floss. I lessened my video bid to one-and-a-half weeks. Tops.

In addition to the get-ups, everyone was now being slopped with mud. One by one the warriors, ghouls, and refugees emerged covered tip to toe in brown slop. Groups of ghouls conglomerated around the two weak heat fans, trying to dry.

Now here's where things started to get ugly.

By this time it was around 7 or 8 o'clock and the sun had gone down. The nice warm temperatures took a nose dive and combined with the night winds it turned freezing cold. Now, wearing rags in 40° weather sucks. But wearing rags in 40° weather covered in mud really, really rots. Not only are you filthy and uncomfortable, but apparently the mud cancels out your skin's natural insulating abilities as well, so we were all colder than usual, without any means to fight off the weather.

Our first task was to form a line by the ship and forge our way through the wasteland carrying packs or flags while the warriors fought each other on the pirate ship. I had a burlap sack thrown over my back. Mundo got to carry a mammoth white flag. After trudging along on cue for an hour, they had us carry this huge, enormously heavy, SLIMY, cold rope over our shoulders. It dug into my shoulder with all its clamminess for a good half hour. After some time we were lead back into the holding cell where we all started to realize that this wasn't such a cool gig after all.

It was about this time that the mud started to crack on our skin. It turns out that the "mud" wasn't actual mud but an alcohol-based "faux-mud" that really started to crack apart after a couple of hours. The problem with the mud was that as it cracked apart, it started to pull on all the hairs on your skin. This hurt tremendously, kind of like a band-aid being pulled off your arm, but every time you moved.

I sat there in the warehouse trapped in my own mud-cracked skin, freezing cold, in great and constant pain, knowing I was only receiving five bucks an hour for this raw deal. I hung my head down in sadness and beared with it. Even sadder was the fact that it was about 12 a.m.

and rumor had circulated that they were going to keep us the full fourteen hours. That meant they could keep us until 6 a.m.! I was thinking it would be more like 2 a.m. or maybe even 3. But 6 a.m.!?! Fuck. Maybe they were creating a virtual hell to get us into our roles.

At about 3 a.m. they took us outside again. This time we were seated out on the fringe, on a log in the wasteland, just out of reach of the bonfires. Every time the director yelled "cut" all the extras coagulated around the tiny bonfires for just a taste of warmth, some tiny comfort in this literal hell. Around 4 a.m. Robin Williams came out of his trailer in a full-length wool coat and started walking around the set. Suddenly everyone slapped their happy masks on, smiling through cracked faces. For Robin's sake. He strolled around talking to groups of extras making jokes that everyone chortled over tremendously, even though they weren't really funny. Not much was funny under these conditions.

Well, at least the guy was cool enough to mingle with us lowly refugees. And at 4 a.m. in the cold. But he was fully clothed in a *full-length wool coat* with nary a painful cracking mud splotch on his body so EXCUSE ME if it was hard to be enthusiastic about his presence. Me and Mundo just sat on our log.

We waited through the night, the cold painful hours dragging on and on like a mutilated animal dragging its body through the dawn. But at long last, the sun finally rose in the sky and it was too light to film this virtual hell any longer.

We were then shepherded to the original wardrobe warehouse where we were to strip and hit the showers and return our rags for our street clothes. Finally the evil torture-mud would be sloughed from my body and drained back into the sewer of hell where it belonged. At long last!

I ran for the shower with several other refugees. We reached its beatific glory only to discover there were only TWO showerheads. For about two hundred people. I was about fifth in line and while we waited we bitched, moaned and waited some more. After a long time, one of the refugees called out from inside the shower. "It's really hard to get this shit off!"

We exchanged some looks and grimaced.

"Please hurry!" someone cried out. "We're freezing out here!"

Suddenly the other girl in the shower shrieked. "The water! It turned cold! It's freezing cold!" and ran out in her towel. The refugees exchanged horrified glances.

"Nooooooo!" someone screeched. "How can they do this to us?"

"Hey, you're getting your five bucks an hour," I joked, driving the nail in the coffin. I was beyond pain, beyond sensation. I had long since left this world and passed into an alternate universe in my head where my body no longer existed – just shuffled it around like I was the walking dead. I started to laugh. It was too absurd. Too pathetic. I laughed as I hit the cold, cold water. I laughed as I couldn't even begin to wash the caked-on mud off of my body and laughed as I saw the thick sad clumps of mud permanently glued to my hair. I laughed as I ran out of soap and as I left the shower with almost as much mud stuck to me as before and when I noticed the mud had turned my blond and black hair a mud beige. And when the woman at the checkout desk told me what time to report tomorrow I laughed and laughed and laughed. "Not on a cold day in hell!" I said. She didn't think it was very funny. All humor had left the building. She shot me a bland look, signed my paper and sent me on my way.

Outside I looked at the sun streaming down on us. Heaven. I was finally in heaven and out of Hollywood hell. It was 7 a.m. and soon we would be at home dreaming away the day. Light was our freedom. We raced down the freeway chasing the giant sun.

Bell Telephone Gig

Did some extra work on a telephone company commercial today. I received the call last night from the casting company asking me to show up at 7 a.m. dressed like a "hip computer nerd." I was stoked because commercials are the best gig in town paying $300 a day on average. BANG. There's rent. What a hook up.

The next morning I woke up at 6 a.m. (ouch), grabbed my nerd glasses and *Shaft* pleather coat and hit the road by 6:30 in the dark. I showed up at the restaurant where we were supposed to "surprise" a co-worker at the telephone company with a party. Upon arrival they hooked us up with a full free breakfast - croissant sandwiches, hash browns, yogurt, fruit, bagels, muffins, donuts, and all the coffee you could drink. You name it they had it. All you can eat is just a perk of the job. I stuffed myself sick and hung out reading for two hours on their dime until they called us inside.

In the restaurant, we were placed at random positions around the festive, decorated tables with the instructions to "act natural," like we were really at a party yucking it up with our work pals. Some people got to hold fake booze-filled glasses and we were supposed to laugh, look happy, and chat it up.

At jobs like these you never know what sort of people are going to show up. You never really know with these actor types and this was a rowdy bunch. We got into a partying, festive mood, cracking jokes and making such a ruckus during the rehearsal that the exasperated director actually threw up his hands at one point. Nothing could shut us up.

Finally the real deal came about and we had to be utterly silent and pantomime our gestures and conversation while the main actress did her opening shpiel. Two guys kept trying to make me laugh during the segment. This one actor who looked like Shakespeare with a handlebar moustache turned to me and in an English accent whispered, "I'm wearing a bra and panties," right in the middle of the filming and later asked, "Don't you just *looooove* the feel of cashmere against the toosh?"

During the next run-through the guy in back of me bent over, nonchalantly put his hand on my shoulder in the middle of the silence and whispered, "I'm constipated." I was laughing so bad. It was tough to keep a poker face with all these shenanigans going on.

In the next part we had to yell, "Congratulations!" when Joe came strolling in the front door and then pat him on the back and so forth. We assembled ourselves around the cake and yelled, "Congratulations!" about twenty times on cue. Although we were beyond enthusiastic at first, patting Joe and giving our most sincere smiles and congrats, by the fifteenth time we were weakly yelling, "Whoo whoo," and mumbling, "Congrats dude." Sometime during the filming someone from the back of the crowd yelled, "You the man! You the man!" Someone else yelled, "Congratulations Joe!" then added, "for stealing my promotion behind my back you little WHORE!" I couldn't believe I was getting paid hundreds of dollars to stand here and whoop and holler with these clowns.

Sometimes at these things you work very long hours – between ten and fourteen hours is pretty standard. Of course you get overtime after eight hours but no one likes to hang around much longer than that. But today they let us go at noon. Only five hours! And most of that was spent standing around reading and eating bagels from the food cart.

The funny thing was a lot of the actors and actresses were bitching and moaning about how hot or cold or tired or bored they were as though they had completely forgotten that they were being hooked up with the cushiest ride in town. Personally, I want to do more of this TV/ movie bullshit. It's like "Come on down and hang out and do basically nothing for eight hours and we'll give you a buttload of money." That's my kind of gig.

Sin on a Dime

Living an artist's life – there is no other way for me. I tried the 9-to-5 thing for years but it left me miserable. I walked around sullen and mean. Working retail and having to deal with all that petty nonsense, I started hating people. Not wanting to go out anywhere where I might run into some of them. Loathing all of humankind wasn't my idea of living.

With the year 2000 approaching and everyone scrambling around preparing for its devastation and ensuing economic crash, I figured it was not only time to find a better job but a more secure one as well. I decided that the safest bets involved either booze or sex. I mean those industries seem to survive, and even flourish in hard times.

I tried to get a job bartending but I didn't know much about all those fancy shmancy drinks – I'm a straight up whiskey kind of girl – so I pretty much ruled that one out. But a sex work job, few hours, big pay – well, I knew I was on to something. And the oldest profession, the sex industry, hasn't waxed or waned much in the past few thousand years. In fact, its profits originally built the whole city of Seattle and its education system. I was sure it could do something for little ol' me.

Instead of wasting my time on this planet, I decided to do something about it. I needed time to sort out my life. Plan my next move. To work on those creative projects that had been collecting dust while I worked my ass off for pennies. To write music. Words. Volunteer. Do something meaningful. I needed time and money. The answer came from a tiny three-line ad in the back of the newspaper.

It said FANTASY MAKERS needed for adult phone line. It was a job doing phone sex out of your home. Moaning for Dollars. It turned out to be a great job! I mean the pay wasn't all that. It sounded good – $25-40 an hour – but you only get around two hours of work out of a seven-hour day, which turns out to be around $60 a day minus that evil, evil tax. But when you get right down to it, it's either art or bucks in the end and for me there is no choice to be made.

The phone sex job was great because it allowed me time. Much of an average workday is downtime, which allows you time to get things done in between calls. Needless to say my house was cleaner than ever, I read more books than ever and finally, finally was writing every single day.

I got into a groove with it. I could type a few paragraphs into a computer, stop, talk dirty for a few minutes, and pick up where I left off. Sometimes I could even do two things at once, mopping the floor while moaning in ecstasy. Type, talk, type, do dishes, talk, sleep, talk, read, talk, read, pick up the guitar and work on a song. The seven hour day passed like that. It was easy to talk the talk for a couple hours if it meant I could own the rest of my day.

The other perk of the job is that you can set your own hours. I mean absolutely whenever you want. Of course for a night girl like me I wanted to start work after noon. So every morning I woke up at ten, got out of the house to get coffee and to write for at least an hour before I went back home to work. Just this simple free time in the morning allowed me more happiness then I had felt in years. Suddenly I felt like life was more worthwhile. I started liking people again. Going out on a voluntarily basis.

The downside is the money struggle. It's a struggle to live in a city that is increasingly less accommodating to artists and writers who earn $60 a day. But I found I am happier struggling than if I deny who I am. Deep in my blood, stamped on my DNA I feel my purpose in life is to write and to make music and when I am not writing or making music I am just walking the planet taking up space. I feel as if I don't exist when I'm not creating something. It's who and what I am.

I got into cheap entertainment. It's surprising how much is out there for next to nothing when you really look for it. Walking out by the beach, around town. 99¢ video rentals down the street. Cheap twelve-packs of beer. In addition, being in a local band earned me some free drink tickets in exchange for our shows. Free or cheap punk shows. A cheap used bookstore on Church and Market Street. Free spoken word night at the local bars The Chameleon or Paradise Lounge. Hanging with friends. And of course there was my boyfriend Mundo who was an all-in-one entertainment system. We could entertain each other for hours in one way or another cruising the town, talking, listening to records, horsing around and other boyfriend stuff. He used to call me at work at various times of the day and breathe heavily into the receiver like one of the callers when I'd pick up.

The drawback to taking the alternative path is judgment. Suddenly I became this pitch black sheep in a crowd. While everyone talks about their daycare or cafe counterperson positions I have to say, "I talk dirty for money." You could just about hear "sex worker" drip out of some peoples' mouths like dirty cum seeping out of a palm. Sex work of any kind is simply against the norm of society, even for people who think they're alternative in thought. Telling people I was a phone sex operator was met with mixed replies. Most people would sort of laugh. Guys would say, "Heeeeeyyy, that's pretty cool!" Then proceed to launch into a profuse denial of ever using one of those services - except when they were fourteen years old and called with a bunch of adolescent friends - just for laughs. Saying how only perverts and hard up guys called *those* things. Stories about how other guys, even ones they knew, got off on phone sex but how THEY would never ever call one of THOSE lines.

Bullpucky. Just who did they think they were talking to? Did they think I fell off the turnip truck yesterday? This was my line of work. I knew the truth. I knew that every type of man from every possible walk of life was capable of calling a phone sex line. Lots of them were the straightest most average Joe sort of guys. I knew that if a lot of guys didn't call 'em, it was probably because they couldn't afford to or were too afraid of getting caught by their girlfriend. Or maybe they preferred a more visual sort of sexual thrill.

But I mean phone sex couldn't be a more nonthreatening form of porn - except for the cost factor. It's totally anonymous. You can't even see the person and it rarely gets past a certain personal level because it's just a voice in the receiver, mixed with the callers imagination and his own fist. Safe sex. No harm. No foul. No cheating. As long as they don't get addicted or too attached to the anonymous voice. Putting a real person with a real life to the voice. That's when it gets ugly.

And that's where things get mixed up - because there is nothing more profitable for a phone sex operator then an addict. Or someone who thinks he is connecting personally with the operator. Sometimes I felt like a scam artist. Like the bait on a hook they're never gonna bite. I made a good chunk of my living feeding men's sexual addictions. It's hard to feel good about it. But hard to feel bad too.

I told my parents I was doing telemarketing for the San Francisco Ballet when they asked what my new job was. I felt kinda bad lying about it but, well, it wasn't exactly lying. More like bending the truth. I did work on the phone after all, and, well, I dressed men up in tutus all the time so it was sort of the same thing.

Well, alright, maybe not. But it's all a dumb job in the end anyway, isn't it? Your time for a flaccid paycheck. And I thought I'd spare them the sordid truth of what my life had become. To them, if I wasn't spending a forty-hour work week making someone else rich off my backbreaking labor, then I was a shiftless bum. They didn't need to know that's what I had become, running from the 9-to-5 gig as fast as I could with all those dreams strapped to my back.

Fueling this engine was a lust I couldn't smother under a pile of papers or a cash register or an important uniform. Life was fucking *now* and I was going to live it. I wanted to take the bull by the horns and ride it until I flew off or rode that fucker into the ground.

The bad girl. The black sheep. The voice of Mary Magdalene. My sin was just beginning. It was worth every filthy dime.

Carnie Code

This man calls up and tells me he's a carnie. Seven years in the biz. He describes himself: 6'2", long red hair, mustache, tattoos. Says he's a real "wranger" and tells me that's the carnie term for hostile. Thirty-two years old, says he can bench press 350 pounds. Been to prison twice. Now he works the Tilt-A-Whirl in a small traveling carnival.

I ask him if he likes his job. He says it's okay, he gets to meet lots of different girls. Knows girls in every state in America. "Yep, we-hell, lemme tell ya, I get plenty a tail." Then says, "Hang on a minute while I blow my shnozz." He honks his horn and says, "I'm back! Did ya miss me?"

"Yeah," I say at a dollar a minute. "I missed you."

Then he tells me he has a gun. He's gonna use it on his boss one day and take the cash and run far, far away. Mexico maybe. He can always work a Tilt-a-Whirl down there. "Some things you don't need a language for," he tells me. "A big gun and the carnie code are all you need."

Tasmanian Sex

Today I got a real wing-danger of a call. This guy with a high-pitched nasal voice calls rattling away like a runaway train saying, "Oh! Heh, heh, I got a Tasmanian Devil tattoo... ON MY GROIN! Heh...heh...Hey! You know what? You know what? Heh...heh...Know what I'd like to do?"

"What?"

"I'd like to, heh, heh, take a peeled hard-boiled egg, yeah, yeah, an egg and... put it inside you! Heh, heh. And then you'd SHOOT IT OUT!... INTO MY MOUTH! Oh! Heh, heh... and then after that you know what?"

"What?"

"Heh, heh, you'd kiss me with a mouthful of CHERRY JELL-O! Heh! Heh! CHERRY JELL-O! Heh! Heh!"

The minutes wiled away like that, the clock ticking like the sound of quarters clacking together and like the sound of cherry Jell-o squooshed in a dirty mouth.

4:45 Friday Afternoon

The phone rings. It's a man who sounds very sad. He tells me he lost his wife many years ago. I tell him I am sorry and just listen. He asks me to undress and wants to run his hands over my body. He wants to kiss my neck. My fingers. My toes. My legs. Between my legs and pretend it's her. I let him do anything he wants and try to sound like a woman his age. Like her.

After a few minutes he says, "Thank you," very quietly and hangs up. Some days I am a $2-a-minute substitute for love.

Little Salvation

Today I woke up. Picked up the phone to call in to work. Slid to the edge of the leopard bed and picked up my guitar. I woke up with this blues song in my head and my fingers felt possessed. They moved up and down the neck on their own, picking and bending like a little dance with the devil, while I waited for the first call of the day.

Sitting on the bed I shook all the demons from the walls. The music overcame me. Swallowed me. It was like being out of body. Finally I felt free of the gossip that surrounds me. Free of the bullshit in the music scene. In the writing scene. Free of my inner demons. Free of my past. Sometimes salvation has six slim strings and a band of ghosts at your back. It's that place where time is lost and nothing matters but the soul.

Cheese Curls

Talking to a guy at work today, I was in the middle of it going, "I want to take a bite of your big BEEF JERKY, baby!" when I heard this sound:

crunch crunch crunch on the other end of the line.

"Oh yeah, yer throbbing ramrod is soooooooooo *hard* !"

crunch crunch crunch

"What're ya doing, baby?" I finally asked, dying to know.

"Oh, I'm just eating my cheese curls," he said like he was explaining the weather in Nebraska.

"Oh," I answered, resuming my suck and fuck wordfest trying desperately not to laugh while I pictured him in his living room beating his shlong with one hand and holding a handful of Cheetos in the other.

Pink Pajamas

Working the late shift is when the real wingnuts call but that's when the best money is to be made. Two nights a week I sat on my leopard bed reading while the rest of the world slept, waiting for the next call.

This one dude used to call me every Thursday at 1:45 a.m. on the dot. We'd run through the usual number and then he would say, "Can I sing you a song? Please? Can I?"

"A song? Uh, sure." I'd sit back and listen while the minutes ticked by.

Then he would bust out:

"I wear my pink pajamas in the summer when it's HOT!
I wear my pink pajamas in the winter when it's NOT!
And sometimes in the springtime and sometime in the fall
I jump between the sheet WITHOUT NO JAMMIES ON AT ALL!
Glory glory HAL-LE-LUUUUUUUU-IA!
Glory glory HAL-LE-LUUUUUUUU-IA!
Glory glory what's it TOOOOOOOO YA!
If I jump between the sheets WITHOUT NO JAMMIES ON AT ALL!"

"Oh, that's FUNNY!" I'd giggle every goddamn time as though I hadn't heard it every Thursday for the last two months. It would go down like that. Then he'd want to get back into the sex thing. The same thing every time. He liked to give me hickeys on my butt. One on each cheek "so the other one didn't get lonely." Then he wanted to spray whipped cream on my cooch and lick it off. Then when he would get ready to come he'd scream, "GIVE IT TO ME! GIVE IT TO ME!"

Then he would beg me to send him a pair of dirty underwear. I said I would if he sent me that pair of pink pajamas first. I gave him the friend of a friend's post office box just in case. I thought it would be funny.

He called me every Thursday, again and again for weeks. Those pink p.j.'s never came.

Morning Hijack

Walking down the street this morning I saw my freedom sitting in the road. Parked by the curb sat an armored car with several million big green ones sealed inside its metal tomb. The guy getting out of the car looked like Rambo - half as wide as the truck with rock formation biceps and dragging knuckles.

I walked up to him. "Hey," I said. "You and me, baby - we could be in Rio by 9 o'clock."

He smiled but didn't take me up on the offer.

Porn & Sneeze

Today this guy called and wanted me to sneeze over the phone for twenty minutes. No shit.

No dirty talk. No moans. No sleaze. All sneeze.

I got paid seven bucks to sit there on my bed and sneeze over and over until he popped his cork over my assumed hay fever. Hey, if men can get off on being swaddled and spanked in rubber underwear, then why not reach Nirvana over a little nasal congestion?

I picture him at home on his couch with one of those nasal strips strapped on his shnozz, imagining his own cum shooting out like mucus – an empty bottle of Vicks Formula 44 rolling on the floor.

The Fantasy Maker

My year working as a phone sex fantasy maker was, I can honestly say, the most creative experience of my life. It's an acting job, really. And that year talking for hours over the phone to perverts nationwide taught me to be an actress extraordinaire.

If you came over to my house that year, you'd have seen a spiral notebook next to my phone. A little journal of sin, page after page of naughty encounters – five minutes, ten minutes, half an hour. All the guilty names and numbers inside.

Phone sex introduced me to a bizarre cast of characters. I had to be so many different people in one day – blond and busty Playboy bunny one minute, a tall dark she-male the next. If someone wants a fifty-year-old cross-eyed bisexual dwarf, then by gum I'm a fifty-year-old cross-eyed bisexual dwarf for ten minutes. White, black, Asian, Latin, naked, fully clothed, small, tall, thin, obese, old, young, blond, brunette, redhead, virgin, vixen, whore.

I had one regular who wanted me to put a pair of pantyhose on his head and ride him around like a dog for half an hour. Another guy wanted me to be an old lady with thin lips who paddled him with a cane. Another caller specifically requested a homely, chunky lady with short brown hair, sagging breasts, wearing suntan pantyhose.

Another guy was a flasher who liked to expose himself in public – especially by the side of a road or freeway. He made me call his penis his "peter" so I'd have to exclaim: "Just look at your *peter!* Good god! You're showing your peter to *everyone!"* for ten minutes.

One of my favorites was a regular caller who wanted me to be an older woman named Betsy Ann who caught him going through her dirty laundry. I'd walk into the bedroom and find him sniffing around in the hamper and screech, "What are you doing with my dirty laundry?! What are you doing in there?!" He'd have a pair of Betsy Ann's old lady nylon briefs over his head and I'd go, "Are those my underpants on your head?" Then scold in my best old lady voice, "You naughty, naughty boy going through my filthy undergarments!"

My best regular had a foot fetish so I would describe my tiny curvy feet, with little cute bulby toes and how I was painting the nails slowly from base to tip with cherry red polish. Another regular guy wanted me to be a female bodybuilder and throw him around and crush him like a walnut in my nutcracker thighs. Another wanted me to be an aerobics instructor who worked out on the Stairmaster in the nude.

Once a hick dude from the sticks of bumfuck nowhere called once asking for a nice Southern girl. I copped the best Southern accent I could but almost lost it when he started drawling in a painfully slow Southern monotone: "Now... I'm... fumblin'... your... breasts," as though he were watching a football game. And when he was about to unload stuttered, "Now...I...am...about...to...EX-PLODE!"

Another guy liked to lick the sweat off of girls' hairy armpits. A business man once called wanting a personal secretary to sit on his lap and do intriguing things to her with a stapler. Some guys liked group scenes, she-males, liked to be dressed up in drag, taken outside and publicly humiliated. Forced into having sex with other men. Told they are worthless repulsive slime. Pissed on, flogged, tied-up, given water torture, foot fetish, hand fetish, dirty laundry fetish. I delved into every perversion imaginable.

The job is not for everyone. I mean you have to be capable of having men call up and say, "I'm wearing my grandma's panties right now." You have to plainly be able to say things like, "I want your hard little penis, Tom!" over and over for five minutes without cracking up. Or try to sound like a vibrator or like you are smoking a cigarette or slapping your own ass or peeing in the toilet or whatever oddball request is asked for that particular day.

Of course there were a lot of average, unimaginative calls – someone who wanted lascivious talk with the girl next door or a teacher/student thing or just a plain ol' blond with big boobs sitting in a hot tub in a bikini. That's when I could really work my magic as I found ways to blow their minds with words. It was in my best interest to get 'em off as fast as possible since they prepaid for the call. Plus it was more interesting for me. I got paid the same if I talked for the full ten to fifteen minutes or if they hung up within thirty seconds of the call. I got it down to where I could do it in four or five minutes on average which increased my time versus money ratio.

And I'll admit it. Sometimes I liked it. Every now and again some guy with an amazing deep rich voice would call. Telling you all the things he'd do, starting by massaging your feet all the way up to your neck. Taking his time, flipping you over, bending you this way and that. Some guys were so nice. So thorough. It's nice to know that there are still some of them out there. Some who aim to please.

The roommate factor is another consideration in the phone sex scenario. A few times my roommate would bring people over to the house in the middle of the afternoon and I know they could all hear my moaning through the thin walls. Somehow it's easier to do the time without witnesses to the crime.

Phone sex was a twisted little window into life. A wild danger ride without ever leaving my room. Days sitting by the bed, by the phone. The walls breathing sounds of perversion.

Spilled Luck

It was one of those days where you wake up and spill everything. It started when I spilled coffee down my leg, inside my shoe and down the stove where it spread out on the linoleum like an oil spill. After mopping that up, spilled cat food everywhere from a chewed-through hole in the bag. Then spilled the dishes in the sink, spilled my glass of water. When I went to buy a burrito down the street I spilled my change all over the counter. When I ate it, beans poured out of the burrito and tumbled down my shirt. On top of that I lost my car keys and my cat chewed one of my favorite shoes beyond all recognition. It's great to be alive.

When I jump-started my old '64 Ford, it overheated within ten minutes, as the radiator erupted its water onto the pavement at a stoplight across town. After I filled that up, the transmission lost its fluid at a slow trickle that day in a red stream that trailed behind me wherever I went around the city. When I stopped to refill the trannie, the fluid spewed out of the bottle all over my hand. No towel. Fuck.

After I staggered home, beaten down, I dropped my house keys on the front porch. Then spilled my mail in the main hall. I tripped up the stairs and when I got inside my cat had torn all my posters down and was lying in the center of their paper corpses shredding them in his teeth. Some days life is a motherfucking bitch.

I went on that day to spill the newspaper, a pile of books, dropped my pen twice, some of my clothes fell haphazardly off their shelf. The trash bag broke when I carried it down and when the day was done I threw my cat out the window, sat on the roof and spilled a bottle of whisky.

About the only thing I didn't spill that day was blood. I feel lucky already.

Played Straight

Las Vegas. The city of glitter and glossy dreams. Where the emptied pockets of thousands light up the neon sky. Where the ghosts of the broken haunt the casinos and the bright sprawling highway of paved money. Where lost souls try to stuff the empty spaces inside with dollar bills. The one city where you can cruise in with a pocket full of cash and ride out on a chariot of gold or drag yourself home down skid row on your hands and bloody knees, leaving a trail of quarters and despair behind.

I'm a real high roller. Yeah. It's all slots and quarters for me. On my last night in Vegas, I won fifty bucks at MGM and twenty at the Luxor, so I was walking tall by the time we sauntered on into the bright chaos of Circus Circus at 2 a.m. I held my winnings in a big plastic cup, three hundred quarters weighing me down like a ball and chain of chance.

We were really tired so we fired ourselves up with some coffee at the Pink Pony Cafe and got back out on the floor. It was 3 a.m. and the place was pretty deserted except for a few diehards sagging over their slot machines, feeding quarters into the machines' metal lips, pulling the arms back weakly.

Within a half an hour I had blown half my cup of quarters. I became insane. Desperate. I threw quarters in two at a time to make up for the loss, changing back and forth between machines, cursing the bars and cherries. Every now and then some small winning would come up and the nasty machine would dribble a few quarters back at me like a tease. But it wasn't enough. It was never enough. I was used to winning, dammit, and the Wild Roses machine was sucking up my quarters faster then I was downing my drink.

Then a terrible thing happened. The quarters were gone. I looked down into the plastic cup and it suddenly seemed huge, vacuous with space. I even pathetically scooped my fingers around inside the plastic to be sure. They were all gone.

I looked around at all the old slot jockeys in elastic waist polyester slacks. It suddenly occurred to me that maybe these people had lost everything and now had to buy $9.99 pants from the backs of junk mailer inserts.

Then I did what I swore I would never do. I dug into my wallet and pulled out my last twenty dollars. I was a wreck. I shuffled deadlike up to the change counter like a prisoner walking to her execution. The guy at the change counter grimaced at me sadly when I handed him the bill. He handed me a $10 roll of quarters and I shuffled back, pale, dark circles around my eyes and my hair sticking out in all directions.

I started getting possessive over my machine. *My* machine. I felt it owed me something. I sat down and dumped in the entire roll of quarters in ten minutes. Then I trudged back to the change counter with my last ten dollars. He took my bill and gave me the roll of quarters, shaking his head at me as he turned away. I felt like a chump but I couldn't help myself. Las Vegas had his hand tugging on my wallet and I couldn't fight for it back. I was totally seduced, laid back on his velvet bed and at his mercy. I had to have those quarters. If I could have shot them up into a slot in my arm I would have.

I watched those quarters leave my fingers. I watched myself pull back the lever as if watching as a ghost from across the room. I watched a few quarters spit out onto the tray below. I watched as I picked them up and put them back into the machine as if they belonged there. I watched as the last quarter left my fingers and as a losing hand fell into place. *Click click click*, YER DEAD.

I felt myself sink into depression. I felt hopeless, worthless and lost. My face was hot and tired, my eyes sunken pits like those of the jackpot cherries. Around me the slot machines looked like faces, the windows bizarre changing eyes, the deep metal trays like gaping silver mouths. Their *ching ching* song like a carnival laugh. Around me I saw clown faces on the walls. Circus Circus and I was the clown, the fool who got taken for a ride in the house of fun. The house of money.

I trudged over to where my friend was on the other side of the row of laughing machines. She was talking to a man who had cuploads of quarters. They were talking, laughing, pulling away at their levers, not caring. Having fun.

I plunked down sadly next to them and the man took pity on me and graciously gave me a handful of quarters. At first I declined and said it was bad luck to play with someone else's money, but he insisted. So I sat down at the Flaming 7s slot machine and started playing the game again. I gave up my expectations and started having fun just talking to them, pulling the lever and playing the game again in that casino in Las Vegas at 4 a.m.

Suddenly in mid-sentence, all three double jackpot symbols fell into place before my eyes. I won. The machine howled out this loud circus song. I screamed. I had won five thousand quarters. $1250! My friend hugged me. The slot jockeys in the casino started gathering around me. Even the jaded casino workers came over to survey the commotion. Everyone smiled and was so happy for me. I felt famous. Special. I was a winner.

Suddenly I knew what this was all about. I felt the addiction deep in my bones. It wasn't so much the money as knowing you were the winner. It was like your fifteen minutes of fame. I felt like I had somehow beat the system. Overcome all odds. Beat them all with a handful of quarters that weren't even mine in the first place.

When they paid me off, they peeled the bills off a giant roll of money, counting each hundred off loudly. We took a picture of the Flaming 7s machine with me waving a fan of hundreds. I gave my friend a hundred and the guy who gave me the quarters a hundred as well because I felt like he was my angel of mercy that night. Or more frankly, my angel of money.

I walked out of there into the neon night with $1050 fattening my wallet with the mantra *I won I won I won* echoing in my skull. That was all that mattered, that was all that was.

Vegas was good to me, but I don't know why. Lady Luck perched on my shoulder that night like a gargoyle wiping away my tears of despair. I left the next afternoon feeling strong, powerful. I looked down at my swollen wallet, engorged with hundred dollar bills and for once felt like a winner in the jackpot of life. Vegas played me straight.

Pray

It's early in the morning and I can't sleep. I pull the curtains back and look outside. It's sunny but with crazy wind, bending the trees down. I slide off the leopard bed, tie up my hair, slip on some jeans and boots lying there on the floor. I know I have last night's makeup on but I don't care. I have to get out of here. I grab my jacket with beer patches sewn all over it and my writing book and hit the street.

I grab some coffee and walk for miles. Up through the Castro, past the coffee and kitsch shops. Up the steep hill of Divisidero Street through the Western Addition, past the nail salons and wig stores. Outside of Helen's Wigs a lady in pink curlers and acid wash jeans stands talking to the street. There are no people or cars.

I find a little magic shop and walk in, because anyone could use a little magic in these times. Walk around the bat eyes, preserved toads, bones, through the incense smoke-thick air, past the giant wall of jars of brown and green roots and herbs. Bought a Virgin Mary candle. Took it with me, walking.

I turn left down Fulton and walk towards Ocean Beach along the empty streets. The fog drapes over me and the street and all the rooftops. In a few hours I know it will lift like a dirty secret under a veil to reveal the madness, the sadness, the exhaust fumes, the retail drone, the internal rush of all the people in the neighborhood, always going always going always gone.

Walking around the streets has become my ritual. My religion. The cracks in the sidewalk are the little path I weave around into me. The city has a rhythm. I try to match its time with my footsteps like a heartbeat on concrete walking, walking like the beat of rain, the beat of fists, the beat of a thousand engines thumping out a slow choke.

I spend my life searching for answers. Answers I try to find in the street. Walking through the fog makes everything clear. Puts all the pieces of my life into focus. But the pieces fall side by side, never into place. I can't make sense of life. It seems so random, so small. Living in a city hell bent on destruction, deconstruction, self-destruction, and the world gets colder all the time. The worst people prosper, the good people suffer, and I need a reason to go on.

My feet are moving on their own. I have no control. I walk all the way out to the beach. It must be five miles from my house but when I get there I'm not even tired. Fear rises in my heart.

Out on the dunes there is a rock. Smooth and worn from decades of salt water and wear. It is something, maybe the only thing I can trust. I set the Mary candle on the rock and pray that my life will some day make sense. I pray that someday I will not feel so lost.

Under the Boardwalk

When I was seventeen I had a crush on a bass player in a Philly punk band, back before I hit the road to California. He was a small muscular guy with a shaved blond head. I didn't really know much about him, just that I wanted to be closer to him. I had liked him for a long, long time. I found out he was working at a t-shirt shop down on the boardwalk in Wildwood, New Jersey – the Jersey shore – and convinced my older sister to drive us down there for the weekend. I mean I wanted to spend some time with her before I headed out west and well, I also had another agenda. This was my last chance.

Our first day I pulled out all the stops. Wearing a black bikini and dog collar, I "accidentally" stumbled into the shop where he worked. He was unpacking some cardboard boxes of t-shirts on the floor.

"Hey you," I said.

He looked up from the boxes with big brown eyes. "Hey, girl! What are you doin' out here?"

"I'm just hangin' with my sister. Down for the weekend."

He was so nice, smiling up at me. "Stop back tomorrow night around closing time 'cause a friend of mine's having a party. Okay?"

"Definitely."

When my sis went to sleep on our last night in Wildwood, I snuck out of our motel room and walked down to the boardwalk. My heart was pumping, excited, scared. There is something strangely romantic about that place at night. All the lights from the rides flashing down by the ocean, sirens from all the games howling, the tram cars blaring "Watch the tram car please! Watch the tram car!" the colorfully painted sideshows - snake girl, sword swallower, the smell of pizza and french fries steaming through the air and the ocean, dark and menacing below.

I walked all the way down to the t-shirt shop around closing time, but the boy was gone. They said he had left hours ago. My heart fell as though I had lost my last dollar on the ring toss and came home with nothing.

When I was a young girl there was this ride called The Hellhole which was a rotor that spun you round and round so fast that its centrifugal force threw you up against the wall. On the outside was this huge green demon face with spiraling horns that shot a huge spray of smoke out its mouth at thirty second intervals. As a child I used to stare at it, fascinated. I went on it when I was too young and it scared me, flattening my arms and legs against the wall, spinning out of control, so much I felt sick and no one understood.

Walking away from that t-shirt shop, I went by The Hellhole and looked the demon in his red eyes. A huge stream of smoke shot out his mouth. I felt his madness.

But I wasn't about to call it a night and let it go that easily. Not after I'd come this far. I wandered the boards looking for him. Looking for anyone who might know him.

I reached the end of the boardwalk and wandered in the last t-shirt shop that sold punk and new wave shirts along with spiked and studded belts and bracelets. Standing in the center of the shirt racks was a large, muscular punk boy with a dark shaved head and faded tattoos dotted up and down his arms. He looked like a marine in a white punk t-shirt, maybe 22 or 23 years old. He took one look at me and in a thick New York accent said, "Whassup?"

I asked him if he knew the punk boy. "Oh yeah! I know him! I'm going to a party right now where he's gonna be. It's no big deal, just a buncha friends drinkin' some beers. You wanna come?"

"Sure." We walked down the sidewalk and told me he was in a band. Called Break-something. I can't remember. He looked like he could break just about anything he wanted to.

We walked into a party in full swing. People were throwing back Pabst Blue Ribbons, empty cans spilling from tables, a gaggle of big-permed-hair Jersey girls screaming through the halls. He took me back into a small bedroom where we sat on the bed and talked.

After about half an hour, the door to the room burst open. It was the guy from the t-shirt shop. He was holding onto this Jersey girl with a huge mane of blond permed hair and a lavender fringed half-shirt that said 'Menudo' in silver letters with a photo of the band beneath. She did, however, have a slender tan body that was offset by her frosted sno-cone pink lipstick. He saw me and cooly said, "Oh, hi," and sat the girl down on the bed next to us. I looked at him with his arm around her, stroking his shoulder.

My heart sank like a stone thrown into the ocean. I didn't want to be here with this marine guy. I wanted to be with him. It was all wrong.

The muscle dude said, "Come on," and led me out onto the back porch. I had nothing to lose. Before I knew it we were making out on a flimsy lawnchair. My mind was lost, sad. A few drunk girls and guys stumbled out onto the porch laughing.

After a while he got up and led me into the bathroom. He closed the door and we attempted to have sex on a tiny step-stool in there. I was not into it, but didn't know what else to do. I decided to just get it over with. It was awkward. We couldn't get the right position on the tiny piece of wood. He fell limp.

He suddenly pulled out, ripped off the condom and nonchalantly said, "Why don't you just give me a blow job and let's call it a night." New Jersey romance.

I wish I could tell the story of a snappy comeback. Or one in which I said, "No thanks," and made a tidy exit. But this was 1987. I was seventeen. And in '87 when you were a seventeen-year-old girl in Jersey, you didn't realize that saying no was an option. It just wasn't something you learned.

Down on the dirty bathroom floor, I thought of how I could get out of there. I had no idea where I was or how to get back to the motel. After ten minutes people started banging on the door, over and over. I stood up and said, "Awww, we better go."

He pulled up his Dickies and said, "Come on." He led me out of the bathroom. Out of the party. We walked out through the streets of Wildwood. He took me under the boardwalk.

Lying in the sand I heard everything that happened over me. Around me. People's shoes clomping on the boards above us, felt their shadows moving across our naked bodies. Cars rushing by a block south, a rollercoaster roaring. A girl's scream from far, far away.

I felt his big heavy body slapping against mine like a side of beef. A sharp shell dug into my butt and my legs were coated with sand. I wondered about the other boy and what he was doing right now. Probably the same thing as us, only with another girl. I felt empty as the seashell wedged in my ass.

Suddenly the marine guy just stopped and said he wasn't up for it. I said I understood. I did. He sat up and we got dressed. We sat there in the sand, under the boardwalk. The streetlights shone down through the slatted boards, making white stripes on our faces and arms. He told me his dad used to beat him. With a belt. Hard and often. An Army dad. Told me about his shitty childhood. I listened. I felt bad. He said he was thinking about enlisting himself, just to get him off his back.

A cop car pulled up and shone a bright white light directly at us. "What are you doing?" the coppers asked.

The punk guy said, "Oh, nothing. Me and my girl here were just talking. You know, just being romantic."

The cops smiled and said with a chuckle, "Oh, I know that one. I met my lady on the boards just like that. Just you kids take it somewhere else, alright?"

"Okay," we said. We went back to the party. He said he had to go. Gave me his address in New York and said goodbye. After he left I sat down and drank some more beers. Alone.

Around dawn I realized I ought to go home. I was so drunk I literally couldn't see. Another punk guy with a liberty spiked mohawk – the host of the party – was worried about me and walked me back to my motel on the other side of town. Shuffling home, the Jersey streets were a blur of faded neon and moving pavement. I hit the ground once or twice, but the nice boy picked me up and steadied my walk. From the pavement I remember looking up once and seeing his mohawk spikes bent out to the sides in all directions like a bent crown. Like a strange punk Jesus. It made me laugh. When he was sure I was home safe he gave me a kiss on the cheek and let me go. I stumbled up the stairs, crept in the door and fell into bed.

I dreamed I was riding The Hellhole, covered in smoke, pinned down, spinning out of control. I woke up to a knock on the door. It was just after dawn. Through the blinds I could see it was the marine punk guy from last night, standing outside our room. I guess I had told him where I was staying. I panicked. *What did he want?*

My sister woke up. "Who is that?" she asked, irritated. I was totally busted. "I'll get it," I said. "It's just this guy I met yesterday on the beach."

I opened the door a crack and saw him standing there in a mesh camouflage half shirt. "I just wanted to say thanks for listening to me," he said, looking down at his sneakers.

I was surprised to see him. I didn't understand why he was here. I felt lonely, drunk- sick and used. "Write me," he said.

"I will," I lied.

Philly Trainride

Walking to the Philly train, snow coming down. Big flakes like tiny ghosts, almost scaring me. The tracks laid out. A young girl runs to catch it as it pulls away. The train moves on through the haunting.

Black Hole

I came out to San Francisco when I was seventeen. I had just graduated High School back in Philadelphia, but I knew that Philly was not my destiny.

When I moved here I didn't know a single person. I wandered the streets alone for months, exploring, trying to understand myself, where I was and where I had been. That first few months in San Francisco was the most alone I have ever felt. I was a young little punk girl, shy, knowing little about the world, carrying around the heavy burden of childhood without meaningful interaction with another human who wasn't 3000 miles away. I slept with boys just to be close to someone.

I rode buses to see parts of the city I hadn't seen before, spending far too much time looking out the window, thinking, thinking. Too much time thinking to be good for a person.

I lived in the black hole of the Tenderloin, the trashy seedy neighborhood downtown, back when it was cheap to live there. Sometimes I sat in my room and wrote in my journal. Read. Sometimes

I cut myself, rows of slices along my forearms like my little secret pain. I lit candles and talked to ghosts. My dead grandmother. I was sad. I rimmed my eyes in black and wandered up and down Polk Street. At that time it was more of a seedy punk hangout, shared with street hustlers and B-movie drag queens.

I took some art classes at the local community college. I took my sketchbook everywhere, on the bus, walking around town. I had a writing class every Thursday at one o'clock. That's where I met Valon. A Goth girl with the same love of dark things. She was a beautiful Siouxsie-girl – teased black hair, pointy patent leather boots. She starved herself. She was thin and pale. We hung out on Polk Street, walked around Chinatown buying paper lanterns, chopsticks and candle holders. Back at my trashy little studio apartment on O'Farrell and Larkin, we lit votive candles, doing speed till dawn, talking about our lives – her teenage abortion, my lost love, our fucked-up families.

One night we went to the Grubstake restaurant at four in the morning to hook up with an older friend she knew who worked as a waitress there. Stacy was a small little firecracker with bright red hair, a faded Sex Pistols t-shirt and a naughty little look in her eyes. She lived with one of the cooks, a twisted queer boy with dark eyeliner smeared around his eyes and a giant crucifix beating against his thin, sunken chest. They drove us in a big black hearse of a car to their apartment where I saw the two most mammoth black cats I've ever seen in my life. I mean those cats were two feet tall, with giant green eyes that glowed like marbles in the dark apartment. While white candle wax from a black iron chandelier on the ceiling dripped on our heads, we smoked pot until time slipped away into the cracks in the walls and the sun crept through the windows.

They drove us to Grace Cathedral at dawn. We walked through the corridors during the early morning mass, our boots echoing through the church. The thin boy put his hand in a bowl of holy water and hissed like a demon. Everyone in the pews turned around while we slithered out, laughing.

I gave Valon a silver Ankh earring which she wore every day until one night it fell down a space in a manhole on Polk Street. We got down and looked for it but it was long gone, lost in the sewer. Eternal life sinking in the cesspool of Frisco.

We sat on the wood floors of my apartment, lit the room full of candles, lit incense that swirled up and sunk into the walls, into all the punk band flyers tacked up there. Drank jug wine. Sat on the fire escape, smoked pot out of an aluminum pipe looking at all the junkies and prostitutes hanging out like colorful ornaments on the filthy streets. We read witchcraft books, held seances, cast spells, love spells, luck spells, needles and blood sealed in wax - anything for an answer. We both shared an open wound of love and a total lack of direction.

Six weeks after we cast our love spells, my ex-boyfriend flew out from Philadelphia to move in with me. It changed my whole outlook to have a familiar face from back home around. Someone who knew me. He was my best friend. He taught me to ride a motorcycle, we threw eggs at Beemers out our five-story window, helped me flick cockroaches out the window to fall to their five-story deaths, bought a drumset for our apartment (causing our downstairs neighbors to beat on the ceiling with a broomhandle), hung out with other punk couples in the building.

Valon and I kept in touch for a while, until she moved back to Los Angeles to live with some old ghoul friends there. Jim and I moved out of that trashy apartment and kissed the cockroaches goodbye. We made it out of the black hole.

Ghosts

When I was 18, my boyfriend Jim and I used to let homeless kids crash at our apartment in the lower Haight. Mostly they were cool, nice kids who had just run away from their respective fucked up home lives. Abusive or insane parents. Parents who didn't love or want them. I knew how they felt. A lot of them were our age or younger. Young punks like us, new to the city, Midwesterners, estranged L.A. kids looking for a more meaningful life in San Francisco.

During the day Jim worked as a bike messenger while I worked at a coffeeshop and went to the local community college. The kids who stayed at our house would walk up to the Haight district to spare change the shoppers. When we weren't working, we'd all sit around the apartment talking, playing with our pet rats or riding around town on our motorcycles, piling all the kids on the back. At night we'd gather together a few bucks, they'd pitch in some spare change and we'd buy a couple twelve-packs of Weidemans, maybe get an eightball of speed and have crazy parties.

Our other roommate Antoine was a punk who was obsessed with gore films. He had posters of B-slasher flicks around his room: "Basketcase," "Lawnmower Man," The Brood," "Frankenhooker." These classics decorated our pad. He had a few gravestones propped up against an altar of skull candles which he would light up sometime during the parties. By the light of fifty glowing skulls he would sometimes give us makeovers in gore makeup - covering us in fake blood, attaching gashes to our throats and wrists with special putty.

Antoine would let us all in for free at a movie theatre called The Strand where he worked, back before it became a triple-X adult theatre. At the time, they specialized in bizarre cult and slasher flicks and we saw them all for free. It was our favorite pastime: sitting in the balcony well below the upper rungs of seats where pervy old men jerked off daily, smoking joints, throwing popcorn at each other, watching Russ Myers films or psycho gore movies.

When my boyfriend and I broke up, I dated a homeless boy for a while. I helped him score dumpster bagels and we'd talk about politics and changing the world, back when we all thought we still could. I would wash his dirty hair. I thought it was romantic. Then I'd drive him out to the Castro or the Haight on my motorcycle so he could spare change the tourists.

Years later I see some of those homeless street kids around town. Most of them have been sucked into the streetlife world. Squatting abandoned warehouses, sleeping in newspaper tents on the sidewalk. I see them walking around town in dirt-encrusted clothes, half-closed dead eyes, beaten down from too many cold sidewalk nights, hunger and sickness. Some seem almost half-aware of the other life that rushes around them. It's like they are caught in time, suspended in a reality from long, long ago. When I see them around on the street and say "Hi," they don't remember me. They just ask me for a quarter or a cigarette. I give them what I can but it's never enough.

A few others made it through the years all right. One is a rockabilly guy with slicked back hair and tattoos who still seems like that kid I knew years ago. One girl, a sad, sad blonde works a retail job in the East Bay. She's still depressed, does dope sometimes, but seems to have things more or less together. Rumors of others moving to New York, L.A., Seattle. New scene. New lives.

I wonder about the others sometimes. About Brian – the boy who rarely spoke, who just shrugged shyly – who OD'd on heroin. The ones who show up on those missing person flyers who no one has ever heard from again. From the relative safety of my own estranged world, I say a prayer for them and hope some way, somewhere they're all right.

The List

In the late '80s in San Francisco, there used to be crazy parties every weekend. Lots of them. Buildings would catch on fire, whole blocks would burn down. This was before the big earthquake at the end of 1989 which shook us all into submission.

There was a magnitude of parties. We rode the city in search of them in a pack of motorcycles. Motorcycle "Big Daddy" Brian was the leader. Since he had a few drinking years on the rest of us - most of us were barely 20 - and since he coordinated the ride, he was Big Daddy and rode in front and decided when it was time to show up at each place and when it was time to leave. There were ten to fifteen of us at a time piled on five or six motorcycles, and we would crash every party in town.

We had a list. Between all of us and our respective girlfriends and boyfriends, we had our ear to the floor on virtually every happening in San Francisco where booze was in some way involved. The parties were ranked in order of possibility: places with free beer ranked at the top of the list, followed by the order of riotous possibly confirmed parties, with the unsure rumors of parties ranking last.

It didn't matter if we didn't know anyone there, we just crashed, walked in like we were supposed to be there and almost always people were glad to have us. If a party was sagging, we got it rolling. We talked to everyone and shared our beer so we were well-received.

After an hour or so, it was back on the bikes and onto the next party – we didn't want to hang at only one place if there were three more raging parties out there. Sometimes we brought people we met at one party to another, piling them on our cycles and roaring away into the night. Everyone on the block knew when we were coming and going with our many bikes – some of them two strokes – kicking up a combined engine roar like a TNT explosion.

I can't honestly tell you how we drove our cycles drunk as hell and fast as cannons without crashing. Quite possibly it was divine intervention. This was our divine quest.

Of course, sometimes the party would be a small private get-together amongst friends. Sometimes held by yuppies or people twice or even three times our age, but we had no shame. If it was on The List, we gave it a shot. Even in these unlikely couplings, oftentimes people just welcomed us and gave us their booze. So we sat and drank amongst the country crafts with our motorcycle helmets banging and beer spilling on the polished wood floors.

Sometimes the party was a bust. A dud. We'd ring the bell to no reply or worse, to an irate lady in curlers and a robe who didn't understand why this motorcycle gang was harassing her. Whoops. On rare occasions we were denied access or if one of us got too drunk, loud and stumbly, were forcibly ejected. But not often. Mostly it was just one long wild ride through the city.

Like I said before, after the earthquake, the party scene seemed to simmer down. Maybe we all looked into our fates a little closer. Maybe it shook a little fear into San Francisco. It was no longer an immortal party. The earth moved. Our apartments were cracked. Things destroyed. Friends died.

Without the cornucopia of parties, we turned to the local watering hole Casa Loma on the corner of Oak and Fillmore. This place was like an event every weekend where all the locals came to hang. It had all the ambiance – dark lit with candles, a jukebox, pool table, spacious rooms. But the booze was no longer free. Now it was three bucks a pop and it didn't flow all night. They never carded at the Loma but most of us were 21 by then anyway. I was one of the younger ones but had a fake I.D. so I could hang.

Casa Loma kept it all going for a while, but like all good things do, it came to an end. Eventually one of our friends, a shy and sweet guy died – cooked on heroin. I ditched that scene. The Casa Loma closed. People went their separate ways.

I stopped running that circuit but I kept a crumpled List like a piece of San Francisco party history. Back when the city never slept and you could hear the roar of motorcycle engines for miles.

5150 Love

When times are good, the days pass like minutes. Fast and furious. This particular year passed like pulling teeth, each day a sharp new pain. Some years you wish could just be erased from time, even if it meant giving that year up. Just so you wouldn't have to look at its hideous corpse in the past. The year of insanity. The year where every inner fear manifests itself as real. The year you realized there is no such thing as undying love, and those who say they will never *ever* get over you are probably psychos or abusive fucks. So much for Romeo and Juliet.

I had a psycho love in that year of hate. A man who was so abusive it was almost laughable. Obscene. A relationship that defied common decency. One where everything the man said was a series of lies, manipulations, and verbal abuse that ended with him throwing a wine bottle at my head and coming after me swinging a thick glass saucepan. It sounds kind of funny now. His anger was so crazy it seems comical— now that I am safe and away from it. I used to try to reason with him but he was beyond reason. Beyond help. Beyond any shred of sanity. Charles

Manson once lived in the basement garage of his house... I should have known.

His name was Francisco Degato. He was a real charmer. A huge teddybear kind of guy who acts shy and humble when trying to impress a girl but is really a loud and overbearing person. The kind of guy who tips big in restaurants, brings big bouquets of flowers to women, and makes grandiose gestures like hiring a mariachi band to serenade a girl on the street. He sent me page after page of obsessive adorations. I thought he was just a man in love. I was charmed into a stupor.

But soon enough the abuse started surfacing. He was jealous of every man I spoke to. Got angry when I wore short skirts, insisting that I was dressing up for other guys instead of just for myself. He would fly into a rage at the mere mention of me hanging out with my other friends, and tried to keep me from seeing them.

He did the craziest things. He had intense hate for old friends and acquaintances. When he would see one of them on the street he would try to humiliate them publicly, shouting, "Hey, you loser! Where are you going, loser?" I was embarrassed. I should have known something was really wrong when he said horrible things about some of his so-called best friends. Then his anger turned towards me. He blew up for no reason at all. Chased me down the street shouting delusions and insults, drawing his finger across his throat like he was going to slit mine open. I felt sorry for him. He had a bad childhood. I understood. I was totally, terribly stupid. I believed he could change.

Then I did try to get away. When I tried to leave, he would call my house obsessively, leaving these messages on my machine that were so apologetic and sad that I finally called back, and somehow he got me back in the game. I mean, I thought I loved him. He told me it wouldn't happen again and I believed him, over and over. He would call my friends and try to win them back, though they weren't fooled. He knew what to say to me though—had my weaknesses figured out, manipulating me anyway he could. He knew I got no love and acceptance from my family.

His mom would call me and say how she felt like I was family and how she loved me. She would try to convince me to stay with him despite the things he had done. He sent bouquets of flowers with apology notes attached. A slew of his female friends called to "check up on me." They would try to persuade me to take him back, saying what a cool guy he was and how he had said I was like his wife, his family. It was like some kind of crazy cult.

When we argued, Francisco always pulled out the same words to break me down: he could see why my family didn't love me; his family and friends hated me. He would break me down until I cried like a baby, and then take me in his arms and say, "It's all right. I'll be your family."

He was totally desperate for me not to leave him. He even wanted me to have his baby, so he would always have a reason—a legal one—to be in contact. One time he faked a suicide attempt—swallowing a bottle of harmless painkillers, then leaving his door wide open for his roommates to find him—in an attempt to make me feel guilty, and get me to come and see him. In the hospital no less, at his most pathetic and forgivable.

Another time, he showed up at my doorstep, weeping, saying he just found out he has AIDS and needed a friend he could talk to and wouldn't I just come out and talk to him for a moment? It turned out to be a total lie.

I started to feel like I would never be free. I stopped trying to leave because I felt trapped. Getting out wasn't a simple matter of saying goodbye and not answering the phone for a week. I tried to leave so many times. He was so unbelievably persistent, calling me at home, at work, showing up at my door, yelling outside my window over and over, shouting our personal business so loud in the street I was mortified. He would physically wear me down into giving him another chance, just so he'd shut up.

After a while my friends got tired of hearing about his shenanigans. They were frustrated with me for being such an idiot for staying with him, so I stopped telling them. And his friends seemed to think he was the greatest guy on earth. Eventually I felt isolated from everyone and felt like there was no one I could turn to for help.

Then all of a sudden he miraculously started regular therapy and things seemed better. During an unusually long stretch of normality—a couple weeks—I let him move into my apartment. It was the biggest mistake of my life.

Soon after he moved in, the abuse landslided. He started twisting everything around, acting like I was the one with the problem. He said that he didn't know why he put up with me and that everyone thought he should leave me. In the middle of an argument, he would call a bunch of his friends, give them a distorted version of what was going on to rally them around him. Then he'd say, "See! See! They all think I'm right too!" When he lost all self-control, I would turn super-rational. There was nowhere else to go. He took up all the crazy space. He blamed me for making him lose his temper. He would freak out, rage around like a raving lunatic breaking things, and then he would call the police on me, as though I had been the one who lost control. My life got really weird and surreal for awhile, like living in a distorted, twisted mirror world.

I asked him to move out, silently plotting to bail for good, but he refused. Simply *refused* to leave. Then things really turned to hell. Once I was driving to the store and he started yelling about the way I drove. His words escalated into the most mean, hurtful insults: "stupid bitch," "whore," screaming, "You'll never amount to anything. No wonder your parents don't love you!" I drove on silently, listening to every word. I pulled over and calmly asked him to get out of the car but he refused. I parked the car and got out myself. He followed, screaming, down the street to the bus stop. He was loud. I was humiliated. I went back to the car and he followed me inside. While I drove home he kept screaming insults.

Something in me just snapped. Instead of arguing back, defending myself as I always had, I just looked at him calmly and said, "You know what? I don't give a damn what you think anymore. Your opinion means nothing to me. You're just a failed musician trying to make me as miserable as you are." He totally freaked. He grabbed the steering wheel and swerved the car into the road divider. I managed to cut it back with only a scraped wheel well but he was totally out of control. I pulled over and said, "Get out of my car, now!" He refused. He was over two hundred pounds. What could I do? I ended up driving him home in silence.

When we got home he attacked me physically, swinging a Corningware glass saucepan at my head. Then threw a wine bottle at my head. Then he threatened to beat the shit out of me if I changed the TV channel. Like I said before, it sounds almost funny now, 'cause he was so fucked up. All he needed was a wife beater t-shirt and a Coors. Except he didn't even drink. He had no excuse.

That's when I decided finally to get him out of the house no matter what. My physical safety was in danger and he would never, never change. I had stopped loving him long ago. I hadn't a shred of respect for this bully of a man, just total disgust. I finally realized he was just filling up that terrible space inside me, leftover from my empty childhood. Just killing my time.

When I told him to get out of the apartment he fought me all the way, kicking and screaming. He broke the handles off all my coffee mugs and piled the ceramic handles in a secret drawer. He locked me out of the apartment by locking the chainlock when I left, refusing to let me in. This was a situation that required delicate maneuvering. He said he would never, ever let me go. Until the day he died. I probably should have just called the cops at this point, but I didn't want to deal with them either. Instead I tried to be nice, avoiding the apartment whenever I could, working late. But I wanted to keep an eye on my belongings and my cats, so I had to check up on things daily. I knew he was capable of anything. We had separate rooms but at night he would force his way into mine, lying down next to me in bed, insisting on trying to "talk things out." He told me if I called the cops all his friends would make my life a living hell. I believed him. It was a true horror-drama. I was terrified of what he was capable of. I actually feared for my life but knew I had to ride this out until the end.

Finally I called his mom and reasoned with her, begged her to get him to leave. She intervened and convinced him to finally move his stuff out of the apartment. I told everyone I knew what was going on so there would be witnesses if I wound up a missing person story on the ten o'clock news.

Once he was gone, I went out and partied for weeks over my new freedom. I was finally free and would never, ever let him take anything from me again. He had already stolen my trust of humankind. I will forever doubt people at face-value. That basic trust has been stripped of me forever. But I also finally accepted that the whole deal was a hell I made for myself by not leaving sooner. A lesson I would not soon forget.

I asked myself many times why I stayed. Why I held onto love even when it was not good. I realized I had no idea what love really was. I never learned it right and no one ever warned me about the bad guys. I just got thrown into the game and had to figure it out on my own.

I carried around these idealized versions of love. Ideas I came up with when I was a young girl, made up in my head, without a model to build from. Certainly not from my parents. Francisco became that phantom love. He acted those ideas out in his make-believe head and made them real—said he would always, always love me. I mean, who doesn't want to be loved like that? Someone who claims they would die and fight for you—like in the storybooks, some urban fairytale. I wanted that kind of intense love. If that's wrong, then I'm guilty. Guilty of being a stupid dreamer.

After eventually finding real love with someone else, I realized that being in love is like being with your best friend. Someone you can trust and run around and play with and count on. Someone who lifts you up, not pulls you into their insanity. That's love. That's romance. Not the crazy boy who bangs on your door for hours and gives you guilt gifts covered in invisible blood.

I had to learn. Everyone does.

But it wasn't over yet. Francisco just didn't get it.

Over the next few weeks he left flowers at my door. He called me at work over and over, telling me he went to a spiritual advisor and was now convinced that my ex-boyfriend had put on a spell to break us up. Not because he was an abusive fuck who threw wine bottles at my head and locked me out of my own apartment when he didn't get his way. But because my ex-boyfriend put a spell on me. That's why I really left.

Then his mom called me at work and said to listen to him. Said that maybe I could talk to the spiritual adviser to verify the information. I hung up.

Two weeks later he came into the store where I worked with a Valentine's Day card and a tape of sappy songs. Out of morbid curiosity, I opened the card. It said a bunch of mush and closed with, "It's over." No shit, it's over! I had a good chuckle. "It's over." As though he could break up with someone who had already left him two months ago and was already going out with someone else. It was such a sad attempt at control.

Then he wrote my mom a letter. She lives in Pennsylvania and has never even met the guy. Apparently he had thought ahead and had gleaned her address from my address book before he left.

A month later he wrote me yet another letter, five pages or so, saying how wonderful his life was now and how he had finally—after two long weeks—worked out all his problems. He ended the letter explaining how it was okay that he wasn't sending any money for the last three months of bills that he owed me or all the personal belongings that he took or broke because it was petty of me to want them back. Of course!

He ended with, "It's over."

HA HA HA HA. I laughed myself into insanity.

Years later he still sends cryptic letters, calls and hangs up, has befriended my boyfriend's friends, worming his way into my life any way he can. He tries to meddle, attempting to get my band pulled off the bill at clubs, talking mean crazy lies. Obsessive love turned to obsessive hate. I double-lock my doors, my windows, looking over my shoulder for what he'll try next. It's clear that he'll never face the truth. About who he is. Because the mirror is ugly. He lives in his endless song of deny deny deny. He makes it clear to me every now and then that he will never ever till the day I die finally leave me alone. He lets me know he is out there somewhere, watching.

I wanted love that would never end. And now I got it. Like a wish on a monkey's paw. Be careful what you ask for. You just might get it.

The Chameleon

We were sitting around with not much else to do and decided to get some fruity drinks down at The Orbit Room, down on Market Street. At that place they had Electric Lemonades, Peach Schnapps concoctions, fruity explosions in a glass, the kind with a wedge of lemon on the side, a cherry garnish and maybe a paper umbrella. After endless nights of cheap beer we wanted a little alcohol variety. Our favorite watering hole The Chameleon had long since shut down and we were eager for an alcoholic thrill.

We got drunk enough to start putting paper umbrellas in our hair and in every other orifice imaginable. All the fabulous people around us smoked their fabulous cigarettes in their fabulous $400 retro outfits while we flapped our umbrellas and laughed like bats. Across the glow of the table candle, Mundo tied all of our cherry stems into knots with his tongue in record time. When the night was up he could tie one in under fifteen seconds.

I remembered how he did that for me the first time we met. We were at The Chameleon where his punk band had played earlier that night. He popped a cherry stem in his mouth, wound it around in there while I watched, pursing his lips like he was sucking on a lemon. Thirty seconds later he pulled out a knotted stem and gave it to me. It was instant love. Any guy who can do that with his tongue has got to be worth his salt.

Looking back I think he was trying to save face. Just minutes before when we were introduced to each other, Mundo went to shake my hand and somehow spilled beer all over his extended hand in the process. He looked down, totally mortified like he couldn't believe he had just done that. I dunked my hand in my cider and met him halfway and we had our first wet handshake.

It turned out he already knew me and my writing from my old column in Maximum RocknRoll and he was now doing reviews there too. We talked for awhile, hung out, threw beer on the bands together, and then he sort of disappeared. When the show was over I saw him outside with his crazy dreaded blond hair sticking out. I went up to him and said it was cool meeting him and shook his hand. He didn't let go of my hand and we stood there for a few seconds holding hands, staring at each other. It was so instantaneous like it was meant to be. The rest is history, but I will never forget our first night at that show at that club.

The Chameleon closed, like all good things do and it makes me sad when I drive by and look at its padlocked doors. I had so many kick-ass nights there (like the time when on spoken word night I stood on the pool table - shitty drunk - and had a pool cue sword fight with Bucky Sinister after the poetry readings, but that's another story).

Anyways, The Chameleon was so cool, like a trashy seedy bar where anything goes. Or went, I guess. It will always be the place where I met the love of my life. Where I first touched his beer-soaked hand.

Cowpoke Boy

Mundo is a such a hick and he doesn't even realize it. He grew up in a backwards cowtown called Tehachapi, located in Kern County where the pride of the town is an ostrich farm which boasts "ostrich burgers and jerky."

Speaking of jerky... he grew up eating deer jerky on a regular basis, as well as every other sort of jerky product imaginable. I do not understand these people's obsession with dried, salted meats and he couldn't explain it either. He sold sticks of jerky out of a tin can as a child, to raise money for his elementary school. When he told me about this I broke out in uproarious laughter and he just looked at me all innocent and said, "What's so funny about turkey jerky?" He didn't even know.

There were other things. Over the years he had employment opportunities working at a wind farm in town and stacking sacks of steer manure. When he was sixteen, he and a couple friends stole three bales of hay for a local farmer in exchange for a twelve-pack of beer.

With Tehachapi fashion it was all about accessorizing. Down quilted vests, baseball caps with the visors pinched together down the middle like a duck bill, jeans with a faded circle on the back pocket from a well-worn can of Skol's.

The favorite pastime of the town was drinking beer and watching the local high school football games. The high school teachers would drink side by side with grossly underage students at parties and talk about the game and this struck no one as unusual. Playing on the Tehachapi High School football team guaranteed one immunity from punishment by teachers, the principal, or local law enforcement. The vice principal, Mr. Crumpacker, would give football players a slap on the wrist no matter how heinous their crime. Football players would be caught driving drunk, swerving down the left hand lane and the cops – and even the Kern County sheriff himself – would pull 'em over and say, "Just win the game this Friday."

There were some real characters in that town. He told me about two boys, Bishop and Roland, who lived in a trailer in the mountains by the edge of a dirt road. He claims they held frequent parties there and when Roland got drunk he got incredibly violent as well and apparently used to karate kick out all the lights. Sometimes during the parties someone would suddenly yell, " Roland's got out his gun! Get down!" As everyone hit the deck, he'd shoot out the windows with a .22, whooping and hollering.

Another kid, Dale, was a huge bully of a guy who was training for the professional rodeo over in Bakersfield. He used to force other kids to simply run away so he could practice his roping skills by lassoing both of the poor kid's feet, causing him to fall smack on the sidewalk.

Another hulking fellow, Delbert, was also a bad egg. He was so mammoth and huge he once beat up three Kern County police officers who were trying to arrest him. Another time he went to a local wedding reception, got into an argument with the father of the bride and threw him into the pool. To make matters worse, the dad had a prosthetic leg which detached in the fall and floated around the pool. Right at the height of the reception.

There was a heavy metal contingent in town as well. These dudes would cruise around in their Ozzy concert shirts and muscle cars spraypainting pentagrams and "Hail Satan!" on walls and storefronts throughout town. Except they spelled "Satan" wrong. Instead they spelled it "Satin." So all over town, written in bold white lettering was the phrase, "Hail Satin! Hail Satin!" If that wasn't bad enough, one day their leader, a huge lunk of a guy named Darrell got the idea to break into and rob his neighbor's house for beer and drug money. He jimmied the window, shimmied inside and stuffed all the valuables into two large canvas sacks. It was then that he realized he was hungry and decided to make a sandwich before he left. The cops found Darrell sitting on the front porch of the house he had just robbed, halfway through a ham sandwich when they made the arrest.

The Mountain Festival and Parade was the local event of the year, second only to Tehachapi High football games. Folks from all over Kern County would come for miles and miles for this event which, if you ask Mundo, was really an excuse for folks to get wasted and sell corn dogs. If you weren't part of an organized group such as the Elk Lodge or 4H Club, admittance into the actual Mountain Festival Parade could still be obtained by riding in a Cushman golf cart with a keg of beer in the back.

In 1990, while the rest of the nation was buying their first home computers, the city of Tehachapi installed their first traffic light. Apparently this caused quite a ruckus and a celebration was held at the intersection to commemorate the event. Even the Tehachapi High School marching band played. Progress was catching up to Kern County.

Even nowadays all the people at the local bars play southern fried rock - Skynyrd and Scorpions and drink Bud from a can. Some things never change.

My favorite photo of Mundo is one I took when he brought me to this place, his hometown. It's a photo of him standing with his back to an ostrich, waving at me, as the ostrich craned down his long pink neck behind him, his huge beak wide open, just before he pecked him on the head.

I love that cowpoke town.

Beasts

In our twisted little heads, Mundo and I invented all these fake monsters to attack each other with. It started with The Steamroller which rolled over me in the morning back and forth, crushing me piteously under his large rotating body. I fought back with the Lobster Claw, using my hands to pinch him into an untimely death.

This was countered with the Burrito of Death which rolled me up in the mattress to suffocate. I returned with The Blob, a shapeless creature who would simply fling its weight upon its victim, smothering him whilst emitting all kinds of blobular noises.

Then came The Vibrator, an oblong beast without arms who would vibrate vigorously over my entire body. This tactic quickly backfired as I could wrap my legs around this beast and enjoy instead of loathe this weapon of devastation. I countered again with The Prickly Cactus which stuck its hapless victim over and over again with giant fingerlike spines. He came back with The Street Cleaner, an offspring of the Steam Roller that would press slowly upwards making terrible hissing and streetcleaning noises.

There were others, like The Fish Flop, The Big Butt Press, The

Butternut Squash, and the chomping Pac Man. You never knew when a monster would attack. Although first thing in the morning, fooling around under the covers was a likely time to be squooshed by an unseemly blob.

Needless to say, when we were in public we must have looked like a couple of psychotics. Standing in the middle of the grocery store aisle, Mundo would taco me in his jacket shouting, "Burrito of Death!" and I would slip my arms out the bottom pinching the air screaming, "Lobster Claw! Lobster Claw!"

What a pair of dorks.

City Girl

Mundo has a surfer friend, Glenn, who lives in Hawaii up along the North Shore. He invited us to come visit him for a few days, so we saved up our pennies and went.

When we arrived in Honolulu, Glenn met us at the airport. He stood there wearing an enormously large Hawaiian shirt, flip flops, his sandy brown hair sticking straight out all over. He presented us with leis, big bear hugs, and talk of booze. It was like Hunter S. Thompson had met us at the airport.

As we piled into his tiny yellow beetle of a car he asked, "How 'bout karaoke?" This was met with two firm thumbs up and we buzzed away into the Hawaiian night to our destiny. I stuck my head out the window to feel the night and the thick heat rushing in on my face, through my hair.

We pulled up at a tiny bar in the middle of nowhere and as we walked inside everyone yelled, "Glenn!" like some Hawaiian *Cheers* episode.

Glenn instantly grabbed the microphone and started working the room. Eighties hits, disco numbers, getting everyone up and swiveling around. We, on the other hand, just weren't convinced that doing a karaoke number was actually a good idea. Mundo was just humble, but I had my own reasons. But sure enough, after a few beers we reached for the stars.

Mundo picked up the mike and sung "Guantanamera," a song he used to have to sing at family Christmas gatherings as a child. As he opened his mouth this rich, deep voice erupted out of nowhere. The boy could sing! He followed up that winning number with, "Hey Good Lookin'" and "All My Exes Live in Texas." As he sung, I could just see the lights dim, a thick mist pouring through the room as a banner with the name "Mundo" in pink cursive letters unfurled across the wall behind him. I listened to him crooning smooth and sexy like some Julio Iglasias Jr. He was *Teen Beat* material all the way.

I tried to lay low, as not to be pressured into singing myself. But Glenn didn't miss a beat. When Mundo laid his microphone down, Glenn handed it to me and said, "Okay, sister, let's see whatcha got."

Over the next hour I got to fulfill my country singer fantasy, my jazz singer fantasy, and my disco singer fantasy, doing a duet of "Dancing Queen" with Glenn. Everyone at the table kept egging me on, even though at this point I was well over the legal "drinking and doing karaoke" limit.

I don't know what it is about karaoke that makes me gesticulate wildly over '80s numbers. After a few drinks it gets progressively worse. By the end of the night I covered *Flashdance* standing up at the table going through the dramatic motions, falling flat on my face while belting it out in an almost scream that left the audience looking at me in blank stares. They just weren't ready for my version of *Flashdance* at that point in their lives.

I was drunk and loose as a goose. Time to pack up my legwarmers for the night.

We got back in the tiny yellow buzz-mobile and sped off drunk and deep into the sugarcane fields, the sandy roads, the crazy overgrown plants, on up to the North Shore.

The next day we took it easy in the morning, hanging out at Waimea Bay which was just across the street from Glenn's apartment. When we walked on the beach I noticed how everyone was amazingly tiny, tan and thin, frolicking around. I suddenly felt out of place. I was wearing boots and a bikini because I didn't have any other shoes. I sported my city girl tan and body - pale and well, *round* all over, as the sun shrivels from San Francisco. I slathered sunscreen all over my skin to avoid the dreaded "lobster" tan and hoped a little sun would seep through.

We threw each other into the waves, stuffed sand down each others respective drawers and then Mundo got the idea to climb up this fifty-foot cliff at the end of the bay. He ran to the edge and jumped in as I watched, sure he was going to crack his head open like a clamshell, but he didn't. He swam over to me, wide awake and alive, and threw me backwards into the waves.

Then it was off to Waikiki to go snorkeling at Hanauma Bay with plans later to bodyboard down at Sandy Beach. On the drive down, Mundo kept bragging to Glenn about how I used to be a ripping skateboarder when I was sixteen. I pshawed, "Oh, that was *years* ago."

Mundo cut in, "No really!" he lied. "She *shreds.*"

"Oh yeah?" Glenn looked over at me and challenged, "But can you ride the *bitchin' wave,* maaaan?"

"Well," I foolishly told him, "I've had road rash on every inch of my body, so what's a little water?"

Glenn and Mundo looked at each other, chuckling. They repeated, "Yeah, what's a little water?"

We pulled up to Hanauma Bay, stripped down to our skivvies and walked down the hill. We strapped on our snorkeling masks and hit the water. As we got in I was instantly swept off my feet, but was determined to make it out to the larger rocks which were only twenty feet out. My efforts were quickly thwarted.

Although this was supposed to be a wading pool suitable for young children, some descent size waves kept pulling in, shooting water down my snorkel into my lungs causing me to hack and sputter whilst being knocked around. To make matters worse, the ground was all jagged coral so I couldn't put my feet down to catch my balance or even stand up.

After a few minutes of this splashing around I yelled in vain, "Mundo! Heeeeelp! I'm drowning!" while Mundo and Glenn stood on the shore laughing at me.

After a while I yelled, "Really Mundo, help!" So, stifling a grin, he swam out and put his feet right down on that jagged coral and picked me up so I could catch my breath for a minute and saved me from my two-foot watery grave.

It was too rough to snorkel so we shucked 'em and just wore the masks, swimming around a little deeper out. Glenn had an underwater camera so we took shots of us waving at the camera and mooning each other amongst the parrot fish.

Next it was off to Sandy Beach for some intense bodyboarding. Well, I had been humbled by the intense power of a two-foot tidepool so my hopes of doing some sick bodyboard moves had been deflated.

When we got to the beach we saw surfer after surfer wipe out in the violent waves. I decided it might be best for me not to surf at all. At least not at *this* crazy spot.

So I resigned myself to take photos instead. I took shots of Mundo and Glenn riding the powerful waves, crash and burning in the surf. After a short time though, I got bored and decided to just go in for a swim.

Big, big mistake.

The waves at this particular beach are small, but lethal I discovered. I couldn't get past the break to save my life. The little wave monsters kept rolling in over and over, breaking with crazy force. I got out about fifteen feet out when a wave shot up and knocked me off my feet. I remembered to duck dive and thought that would save me. Wrong.

The force of the crashing wave threw me down and pinned me to the bottom. Wave after wave threw me to the ocean floor shooting water up my nose, in my ears with a force I never thought possible To make matters worse, the waves were full of sand which was also forced inside my ears, in my eyes, through my hair, up my nose, down the crack of my ass and every other crevice imaginable.

Unaware of what I was getting into, I had also worn a leopard print bikini that wasn't, well, *snug*. The top of my bikini got completely twisted around backwards in the aqua-force, so I emerged from the wreckage, drenched, covered in sand, my top skewed completely to one side. To make matters worse, a bunch of bodyboarders sat on the shore snickering at me. I was such a sad Betty that day.

Humiliated, I skulked over to the shower. Standing there I attempted to rinse out an endless stream of sand from my hair. Humbled, I lifted my bikini bottom from my ass and let the water run through. A huge chunk of sand fell from my bottoms and exploded on the concrete in front of the many surfers. From my butt crack I rinsed out an amount of sand that must have significantly depleted the beach by a measurable amount.

I washed the endless stream of sand from my body, but could still feel a hunk of sand stuck up my twat that would simply have to humbly remain until a later time.

Back at Glenn's apartment I finally took a shower and with a little soap rinsed all the sand away. I came outside so the heat would dry and warm my hair and limbs. In the sun I looked down and saw that my skin was a light golden brown. The city girl had gotten some color.

While Glenn went for a walk, Mundo and I sat out on the porch watching these tiny green kamikaze lizards who would just fling themselves off the second story porch and sail down into the tumble of leaves. While the lizards fell through the thick heat, Mundo and I had pure unadulterated animalistic sex until the Hawaiian sun peeked his hazy purple head up over the horizon.

The Night the World was Dead

After watching a punk show up at the Cocodrie, Mundo and I stumbled drunk around North Beach, down through the abandoned Financial District. It was so empty it was like the world was dead and we were the only ones left. Mundo lifted me up and spun me around and ran me down the street. I lifted my arms up and for a few minutes I flew. He threw me through the night into a big trashbag of foam packaging peanuts and I brought him down with me. We made out in the trash until I found a sheet of triangular blue cheese stickers.

We had a sticker fight that Mundo won. We had blue cheese stickers on our butts, jackets, hair, covering one eye. Screaming down the streets covered in triangle stickers.

The next day at breakfast Mundo still had some stuck haphazardly to his sweatshirt. What a fucking cool night.

Boas and Booze

It was the last day of the year. I wanted to bring in the new year with a bang. Neither Mundo or I were in the mood for the usual big party scene. We decided to take our chances by just hitting the bars around town and seeing where we ended up.

Time to hit the hooch. We kicked the night off at Trader Sam's, a small tiki bar up in the Sunset district. Trader Sam's features fruity drinks in a festive Polynesian atmosphere, complete with little grass huts you can sit inside with friends. The drinks are always fraught with paper umbrellas with fruit wedges stuck to the sides. We both wanted to go to Hawaii for the new year, and this was the closest we could get. Plus it's hard not to feel festive with a tropical drink and a fruit wedge.

We started off with the infamous Scorpion, my personal Scorpio favorite, which is less of a drink then a large wooden punchbowl full of rum, vodka, and fruit juice. It had four paper umbrellas and four fruit hunks around the sides. Fancy. We drank our bowl of booze and other drinks until we were sufficiently liquored up. This was measured by the number of paper umbrellas stuck in our hair and clothes. Mundo was positively garnished with them. Time to head out.

On the bus ride downtown, all these Irish dudes were standing in the aisles swaying, howling songs and talking shit. One of them leaned over, gesturing towards Mundo's baseball cap pierced with two pink paper umbrellas and hollered, "I hope we're not getting the weather he's expecting!"

The bus roared with laughter. It was only 10:30. The whole bus was sauced.

We got off on Van Ness, a block from one of our favorite bars The Hofbrau where we were supposed to meet some friends Dave, Mike, Dan and Janette. The Hofbrau was a small German bar with a highly mixed age group commingling over beer, our common denominator. Alongside the younger folks, the regular patrons were alcoholic World War II veterans who would relay their war stories to any ear who would listen. It was a friendly drunk place, no jocks or bullshit, where everyone sorta blended in like a strange soup of time.

When we got to O'Farrell Street, we mysteriously couldn't find The Hofbrau. There was a sign that read Koko's in its place. Disappointed, we peeked inside and sure enough it was the same place, same layout, except now it was a Chinese bar instead of a German bar. Well what the hell, we thought, how different could it be?

We walked in. Mike and Dave were sullenly playing pool and slumping around looking painfully sober. There were only about three or four other people in the bar sitting under the homemade, hand lettered "Happy New Year's" banner in the back. Two Asian women were working behind the bar, doting over three male customers who looked like surly Mafia dudes. One of the women glared evilly in our direction, marched right up to us and barked, "I.D.!"

"Okay, okay," we said digging out our cards. "Jesus." Both women were eyeballing us suspiciously. We ordered two beers anyway.

When she went back behind the bar, Dave leaned over. "Hey," he whispered. "I think this is a Mafia bar."

"Or a prostitution ring," Mike added. "This is hecka sketch."

On the upside there was a Chinese buffet spread out on one red table in the back – fried tofu, chow mein, spring rolls. It looked like it was spread out as a welcome for the patrons of the bar, as there was a "Grand Opening" banner hung beneath. Never one to pass up a buffet, Mundo piled his paper plate high, making the best of a bad situation, inhaling the fried tofu triangles and noodles. When went back for seconds, the other lady came over and slapped his hands away, covering the buffet trays with a large brown towel. This was pretty funny as there were only three other people in the bar, all of whom were drinking and totally disinterested in the cold and hardening food. Plus it was a half hour to twelve. It was just going to go to waste.

This was a depressing way to bring in the year. These women wanted us to leave and frankly at this point we wanted to as well. But where to go now? Our plans had been foiled. We took the hint and hit the road.

We tried Edinburgh Castle, a great Scottish bar down the street complete with a bagpipe player, but they were charging a $6 cover that night just to get in. I only had about ten dollars with me and a bottle of $3.99 champagne. That was out. Plus who wants to pay a cover just to enter a bar without even getting a lousy drink in return?

Across the street was the Gold Room, an old-time gay bar. Through the doors we were lured inside by the festive gaudy Christmas decorations. Garland and tinsel, blinking colored lights. A paper Santa on the bar mirror. It looked like a happier place to be. We all went inside and were greeted by a barful of friendly, older daddy type guys. Our young posse of cute guys was well received.

Janette and I were treated as fabulously as queens, given our own special barstools, while a bartender brought out feather boas for us to wrap around our dresses and dog collars.

I popped open my cheap champagne and passed it around. After a few minutes the owner came up to us and said, "Where are your funny hats? We need some funny hats!" He held up his finger and disappeared into the back. He reappeared holding a cardboard box full of New Years eve party hats and tiaras. The guys put on the party cone hats and we put on the tiaras. Mundo somehow got on a party hat and a tiara. Then the owner come out with a bottle of complimentary champagne and poured everyone in the bar their own tiny plastic glass.

Well, this was the life. The ball dropped, we were drunk, silly and sauced. Sometime after midnight we looked over and Mundo was tangoing with one of the daddys. We all took turns and waltzed drunk through the night to show tunes.

Around two o'clock Mundo became very insistent on leaving. He said he wasn't feeling so good. We were tanked, the drinks were about to be cut off anyway, so we said our goodbyes and left stumbling into the street.

We sat at the bus stop. A tall guy leaned against a streetlamp post staring at us. I looked over at Mundo. He looked very green. He nonchalantly leaned over and puked out that Chinese food all over the sidewalk inside the bus shelter. It had claimed its revenge. I patted him on the back, "Get it all out, honey." The guy leaning against the post started laughing hysterically.

The bus came and we got on. To our dismay, the bus happened to have a jerky foot driver who was playing drums with the gas and brake pedals. He alternated between them stopping and starting so that the bus careened forward and violently stopped, causing all the passengers to lurch forward, grabbing for the poles and hand rails. Lurching forward and stopping, lurching forward and stopping until even I got queasy.

Mundo reached up and pulled the cord. We got off and he puked into a bush in front of the California State administration building. Government dissent is always a great way to bring in the new year.

The next morning, I woke up in Mundo's arms. It was supposed to be a new start, a clean clear slate. The first day of a brand new year. But instead the night before was blurry, an underwater memory of boas and booze, tiaras and waltzing and champagne bubbling – all drowned out with hooch.

I sat up and looked back on yesterday. Then looked down at my boots. They were sprinkled with champagne and there were little splotches of puke already hardening along the sides. It was going to be another insane year.

The Shoe and the Man

You can tell a lot about a man by his shoes. Take the Oxford Slipper Man. You know those leather slip-ons, sometimes with a little tassle on top like a garnish? Here's a man who wants the easy life. Gourmet food with a parsley sprig on the side. Just like the one on his shoe. This Slipper Man is a man who wants to slip into his shoes without effort like slipping into his cushy white collar life. A man who likes to lie back in his Italian leather recliner and look down on the peons below doing his dirty work. Manicured hands. One of those faux mini-waterfalls on his desk. A man who thinks he can buy anything. Even love. Which he just may do during lunch hour.

Next we have the Sandal Man. Here's a laid-back specimen in all forms – rope sandals, Birkenstocks, shower thongs – it's all the same. He's a cruise-through-life, has been or is currently smoking weed (hand-rolled, homegrown, quite possibly smoked out of a bong resembling the skull of Jerry Garcia) sort of guy. Has a "carefree" attitude towards personal hygiene, often with an obscene amount of body hair.

The Sneaker Man is harder to call. I mean it really depends on what type of sneaker we're talking about here. The slip-on sneaker guy is a little lazy. A surfer dude perhaps. Definite slacker potential. Any guy wearing those puffy sporty high-tops (unless he's part of the hip-hop scene — that's a different story) has serious jerk potential. It's like a flashy car. Puffy, flashy shoes with racing streaks. Here is a man with something to hide. Perhaps a small penis. But he isn't usually bright enough to hide it. This is a "Hey baby, if I told you had a nice body would you hold it against me?" sort of fellow. Ex-frat boy who hasn't figured out that life is not a giant campus. A guy who hasn't faced the fact that he has already gotten his degree, graduated college, gotten married, spit out his 2.5 kids, and is living in a prefabricated tract house, working at his insurance salesman position, squandering what's left of his weekly paycheck on a sportscar with a grossly inflated sticker price, and the rest on booze and cheap women.

The Converse Man, however, is a good one. But not for everyone. Sort of straightlaced, innocent, nerdy kind of guy but with a funny, kooky streak. This is a currently-reading or used-to-read comic books man. Most probably collects weird toys and/or action figures. One who sort of doesn't want to grow up. But he's a reliable one. The type to have the same lover for three or more years. Sometimes goes after the mother types who think it's so cute that he reads comic books and plays with toys at thirty years of age. This guy is high on the nice, low on the ambition. Thumbs up for the Converse guy.

The Skater-Sneak Guy is a heartbreaker. He wants danger, adventure. He may settle down but he's always got that roving eye that can't be tamed. Can be a loner. Sometimes a straight edge, no drinking type. That particular type makes me nervous. Like they fear the booze is the window to their true self which they want desperately to hide. Overall the Skater Sneaker Man is great for a wham-bam-thank-you-ma'am sort of thing, but generally not a keeper.

Dress shoes - whether wing-tips, creepers or similar fancy deal -

indicate a man who values his appearance. Perhaps above all else. This is a man who spends as much time as his girl fussing over or at least considering his hair. This man looks sharp and you can bet he knows it. He'll play it cool with the ladies, but he's often hiding a deep and sometimes disturbing insecurity. He has definite backslapper potential, an "I'll call ya!" sort of guy. Makes a great band manager or club booker. Often a shameless player. Possible abusive tendencies, but not always. This can go either way. Either he's the abusive sort, berating his woman in private and keeping it all smiles and romance in public. Or he's the complete opposite. The flipside of this shoe is the more shy, needy type. The guy who just wants to look good, 'cause he feels a little insecure inside. The marrying kind. And a sharp dresser to boot.

Speaking of boots, the Boot Man is a man I like. Mysterious. Brooding. Dangerous. Artistic. Independent. A man who doesn't mind getting his hands dirty. Mechanically inclined. A useful guy. Great at sex. In bed this man is all pistons and lube, working your body like a machine. However, a little unreliable. The sort of guy who tells you he'll call at 7 and comes over at 9:30 because he stayed out after work drinking with the guys. Blue collar job. A man's man. The Boot Man is a man who works in the shoes he wears throughout his life.

There are more factors, like the thrashed shoe factor (messy guy) or unevenly worn soles (dreamer) and these qualities don't apply to women – that's another whole topic and don't get me started. But it all comes down to this: If you want to know a man's soul – it's all in the sole.

Party in Oaktown

Twilight falls to night, laughing, talking, friends clicking bottles, beer spilling from brown lips, brother bear-hugs Mundo talking this crazy story – someone just shot his girlfriend's whole family down in L.A. A moment of silence turns to – out comes the whiskey – turns to a wrestling match on the coffeetable, bottles tip and roll.

Room smoke flows like a black dream, joint passed from finger to finger to – people standing around the kitchen table, a heated Domino game. "Domin-o!" screamed out twice, pieces slapped down full palm, pieces break, the table sways, threatening to flatten. More drink, more slaps, laughing loud. Thick heavy music pumps out of the two speakers like two hearts in time with the night. Bodies move and sway. Slap slap slap. "Domino-OH-OH!" A big win. People fade off onto the porch – me and Mundo head to head – a Domino war like no other – slap slap slap!– he quickly wins and disappears into the kitchen. He reappears holding a chicken wing he stole from the fridge – grinning and grooving out– flapping his elbows doing the crazy chicken wing victory dance.

Everyone is gone or down on the couch or passed out in chairs chasing their dreams. We hide away, making out in the bathroom pulling dress up lipstick smears and a cheap feel. Slip out and say goodbye, hit it on out to the long black car, weaving through the downtown Oakland streets, lost, lost, looking for a gas station or some luck. Outta gas. Fuck.

A maze of streets, a little dark dirty station. Dodging tiny dude with window squeegee, rubbing our bumper, chasing Mundo around the car. Fill it up and speed back through Oaktown, back across the glittery bridge and back towards the empty streets of San Francisco.

Waking up to hot sun on our face. Mundo turning over and over rolling over me saying he feels like a rotisserie chicken. It's just another morning after another night of crazy crazy drink. Two lost kids in a lonely town.

On the Mission

When the sun stabs into the city and the wind kicks my hair up like snakes I'm missing you. I feel your breath in the fog that takes me up inside, feel the beat of your heart in me in every footstep on the sidewalk. My whole world is a celebration of you, a memory of drunk on cider, drunk on your body, kisses on the Mission streets. Tangled in the leopard coat falling backwards, falling back into you.

Lush

When you live for the night. When you want the party to go on and on but it never does. Morning always comes to clear your eyes. When you drink and drink and want more and more but it's never enough. When you've lost the meaning in life and try to find it in some broken beer glass on the sidewalk. When you write to find meaning in life and find your meaning in life is to write. They cancel each other out so intertwined spinning round and round it's better to simply drink.

When you drink because people are mean and you want to sink their words in booze. When the bartenders know your name, even when you've forgotten your own. When "just one more beer" turns into six. When "getting lit" starts to involve breathing actual fire with a bottle of grain alcohol and a match. When you start to think the Pepsi-painted public transit bus is an actual moving can of cola. When you write your name in some wet cement on the sidewalk and end up leaving a face plant instead. When you yell and scream because you've forgotten how to cry. When you drink to feel your heart beat like a jackhammer. When you live fast to suck out as much life as possible from a dead dead world. When you start to blend in with the lunatic fringe and you like it.

When things are looking ugly on an early Sunday morning, waking up on the floor, makeup smeared, hair frozen into a spray of bangs sticking straight up and out on one side of your head from passing out on your left side all night. When you remember lining up the tequila shots along the bar last night, your boyfriend throwing a full bottle of beer at a sports utility vehicle, puking in a cab, standing in Safeway raising a fist full of sour gummy worms and the rest is black.

Waking up drinking water like the whiskey last night. Going back to bed because the truth hurts. When your cat sits on the end of your bed, looking at you, looking at you and even he knows you're a lush.

Harmonica Man

Walking down the street today, I saw a homeless man sitting on a milk crate playing a harmonica with a cardboard tip box in front of his tapping feet. It was empty. As I walked by, he played *Amazing Grace* sadly, slowly. I put two quarters in the box. Someone had taken his shoes.

Cobra Bull Cookie

As I was leaving Muddy Waters today, some punk dude came up and asked me if I would draw him a picture of King Cobra fighting the Schlitz Bull over a sandwich cookie. He said it was for his zine.

I told him I had forgotten how to draw.

He said, "That's perfect! It's better when people can't draw!" and showed me snake and bull pictures of those who had come before me.

"Hell, why not?" I thought and scratched out a quick cobra bull cookie scenario. It was a pathetic rendition but he loved it and thanked me profusely. I asked him what zine it was for and he said *Malt Liquor & Cookies*. Two of my favorite food and beverage items. Right on.

Hardware

Walking down the Haight this crusty punk guy asked me, "Can I have some spare change to buy a new necklace?" This was funny because he had about a hundred chains locked around his neck.

"That's a lot of hardware," I told him. "Do you ever take those things off?"

"No way!" he said. "It's my collection. Some people collect stamps. I collect dog collar chains. I have to wear 'em or someone'll lift 'em"

"I hear those are a hot item."

"Yeah," he said. "I can't ever take them off!"

"Never?" I asked.

"Never," he insisted. "I've had these on for six years."

"Six years," I repeated.

You'd think that at least once a year he'd have an annual "cleaning of the neck." I shudder to think of the neck cheese that must have built up under there after all those years.

I gave him the ball-chain around my wrist. "Here's my donation to your cause."

"All right!" he shouted, leaping around. "All right!"

I left him wrestling that thing over his foot-wide metal neck. It gave him great joy.

The Gelatinous Fury

A girl I know decided to raise money for her literary magazine, *Fnord*, by holding annual Jell-O Wrestling competitions. Her wrestling name was Gelatina.

All the crazy folks in town showed up for the event dressed to the nines in various wrestling garb - Spiderwoman outfits, tutus and spiked armbands, glitter bikinis with matching short sets, two-toned capes, clown and space rabbit masks. One man simply had a baseball cap on with a carton of lime Jell-O taped to the front.

The night kicked off with the pre-event Crisco Twister in which several nerdy guys with huge beerbellies in tighty whities slipped and slided around in twisted pretzel positions on the plastic mat, attempting to keep their greasy hands and feet on the colored dots. A man in a burgundy fez spun the Twister dial calling out, "Left foot Blue!" while Gelatina skated around them on her roller skates wearing a tutu, greasing the contestants down with Crisco. When one of the players would slip and fall on their face the crowd would break into an uproar, whooping and screaming for the slippery sap.

Soon enough one person in the crowd spotted a rather large contestant- with major plumbers butt spilling out of his mammoth drawers – and pulled back his waistband, shoved a huge handful of slimy Crisco down the back of his undies, sliding it right down that big exposed crack – and let the waistband snap. Crisco shrapnel flew in all directions into the crowd. People in capes and masks swooped and ducked. All semblance of order was lost as the various contestants dove their hands into the gallon size vats of Crisco on the sidelines and scooped it off the plastic Twister mat, hurling blurbs of white Crisco at each other – *flurp flurp flurp* – white gobs of grease arcing through the air, striking naked flesh with an audible "Blat."

All bets were off – only the back of the club was safe from flying grease, where one could still be embraced in an unsuspecting bear hug by one of the Crisco-coated contestants streaking around the club.

After the Crisco mishap, there was a fire-breathing magic show performed by the be-fezed host of the Twister match, followed by two theatrical bands. It was all entertaining, but after a while the crowd grew ugly. A chant of "Jell-O, Jell-O" rose up from the back of the club, first softly, rising to a screaming crescendo, "JELL-O! JELL-O!" until two guys dragged out the inflatable kiddie pool and started pouring one hundred gallons of cherry Jell-O into the bottom.

The cubes of Jell-O shimmered and wibbled in the stagelights, heightening the anticipation. After we could take it no longer, the girl hosts Gelatina, Annette Funajello, Jell-O Jiggler and others stripped down to their spandex bras and thongs. The ladies, first Annette and Gelatina, slowly glitched into the ring while from somewhere an accordion began to wheeze a twisted melody. It was on.

The frothing women flung themselves at each other, writhing and slopping around, Gelatina quickly pinning Annette flat on her back. A quick victory. Then it was on to the next two girls in spandex leotard sets who ripped one another's shirts off and fell splat into the Jell-O.

Soon enough, people from the audience started shucking their capes and boots and flying into the murky goop, right in the middle of the competition. The accordion song grew faster and faster. It was every man, woman, and freak to themselves. A Jell-O riot ensued. A mass orgy of cherry-coated, wriggling, half-naked bodies piled into the tiny kiddie pool. One man pinned face down under three jellied women nearly suffocated in the gelatinous fury.

Blood red jelly coated the wrestlers' hair, faces, and bodies as handfuls of goop were shoved down bikini bottoms and briefs, mushed in unsuspecting faces. Ectoplasmic arms and legs stuck out from the heaving mass of slick bodies, hurling Jell-O blurbs into the crowd with every kick and shove. Jell-O hunks hung suspended in the spectators' hair, dotting our arms and clothes.

After the event was over the Jell-O people streaked around the club, chasing unsuspecting friends and spectators. They tried to wash the jelly blurbs off their bodies upstairs in the two tiny bathroom sinks. Rumor has it the drains were clogged with the gelatinous remains for weeks.

The Fullest Glass

It was a rainy Tuesday afternoon. I sat inside that trashy Mission cafe Muddy Waters where the hard luck hangs heavy and the psychos are always a treat. I was just hanging out with Mundo when this guy sitting behind us ordered a guava Kern's Nectar drink in a can with a glass of ice on the side. As we drank our black coffee, he sat there for an hour pouring the juice slowly, methodically into the glass, filling it up to the rim. Then he would carefully wipe the sides of the glass, the sides of the can, and the table clean with a paper napkin. Then he would carefully pour the juice back in the can and repeat the process. First wiping the glass, the can, and the table, all in that meticulous order.

Finally after twenty minutes of cleaning, wiping, and pouring Mundo looked over my shoulder and gasped, "He took a drink!" The guy had taken a drink. There was a half-inch depletion in the glass. It was a real moment which excited the man greatly. This variable in The Kern's Nectar Plan really whipped him up into a cleaning frenzy. He began wiping the table at double speed, over and over, then back to the glass. Wipe wipe wipe. And then the can. Wipe wipe wipe. Just in case he had spilled some of the offending nectar onto the table or down one of The Nectar Receptacles.

After he settled down, it was back to the old routine. Pour nectar into glass. Wipe glass. Wipe can. Wipe table. Pour nectar back into can and so on, taking perverse delight in the pouring process, from can to empty virgin glass as if it was somehow defiled after being filled with the thick nectar. Let Freud put that in his pipe and smoke it. All I know is that all this wiping and pouring for forty-five minutes made me never want to drink a guava Kern's Nectar drink for as long as I live.

Sometime later Mundo and I left the cafe, leaving him caught in his never-ending time loop where the tables are always dirty and where the glass is never, never empty.

Streetcar # F

Riding the F train down Market. This homeless dude smelling remarkably like booze stumbles onto the bus around Civic Center. He's got no shirt on and his exposed skin is so encrusted with dirt it's black. He's got these two dreaded ponytails sticking out on each side of his head and a gigantic dog bone weaved somehow into his hair so that it dangles down like an extra appendage. He's got big unlaced combat boots on and he's stomping around the crowded aisle as people swoop and sway to get away from him.

"May I have your attention!" he suddenly proclaims. "I am now officially up for adoption. Picture me in your home!"

The people on the bus laugh or glare at him or shift uncomfortably in their seats. There are no takers of his offer.

"Oh, come on," he slurs. "I'm not that ugly. I'm so ugly, I'm cute!" He leans down to a lady in a beige power suit and whispers loudly, "You look like you'd make a good mother. I'd make a good son."

The train stops and he stands up and shouts, "So who's gonna adopt me? Huh? Is it you?" he says pointing at each person as they step off the bus. "You? You?"

It's my stop. As I walk in front of him he looks at me and says, "You understand." I stand there and just look at him. Then nod and step off.

The streetcar lurches on, leaving the dirty man an orphan.

Cabbie #617

Cabbie #617. When he picked me up on the wrong side of the street he whispered, "Are there any cops around?" before making an illegal U-turn. I told him I was going to the Mission and he told me his life story.

He was a Merchant Marine for forty years, only did cab driving in his spare time. "I gave up drugs and booze ten years ago," he tells me. "Not because I wanted to but because my doctor told me to."

"What did he say?" I asked.

"Oh, I was coughing up blood so I went to the doctor and told him about it. I told him about all the drugs and booze I was doing. You know," he chuckled, "you can lie to your mother or your girlfriend, but never lie to your doctor."

"I had a hole in my lung the size of a pancake," he continued. "So I had to quit. I quit drugs, booze, cigarettes. Just do 'em occasionally. But I'll never quit weed," he said, reaching into his front flannel pocket. "I like the weed." He pulled out a fat joint, lit it and said, "Want some?"

"What the hell."

"When I was in Bangkok, well, there you could get an aspirin bottle size a' coke for two dollars. I tried the stuff once, but it didn't do nothin' for me. Just made my dick numb for a week. I threw it over the side of the ship."

He let me out at 20th and Mission. "You're a cool guy," I told him. "You oughta take care of yourself and live and stop doing that shit."

He chuckled, "Okay, okay," and looked up at me in a way that told me he never will.

Busride #71

Sitting on Muni bus #71 on the way home from work, I notice this young metalhead guy wearing a Metallica shirt turned around talking to his friend in front of me. He's got a shaved head under a red baseball cap with these beautiful slanty blue eyes all innocent and shining, full of light. He looks sort of like an old boyfriend I used to have.

I stare at him but look away when he looks back because I don't want to start something I can't finish. I notice there is something strange about his face, then notice that one of his eyelids is kind of drooping low across his eye, like it is half asleep looking lazily across the world.

It's then that he turns to the side and I see his ear melted in a twisted ball, like a glob of hard flesh stuck to the side of his head. I realize that is why his eye is so messed up. I realize that is probably why he thinks I am staring at him, not because of his slanty eyes. I look at him and feel so much so suddenly because he is so beautiful even with and maybe especially because of his twisted ear and sleepy eye and it's then that it's my stop and I get off.

I step off the bus and start crying like hell and I sort of know and I sort of don't know why but just walk home in the fog sobbing for one of God's mutilated angels in a Metallica t-shirt.

Red Man

There's the red man again, walking by me on the street. The red man is this red "devil" man who slathers red paint all over his body, wears a red shirt and trousers and thinks he's Satan.

Today he's wearing a suspicious blue '70s ski parka over his usual red garb. I guess the devil is a bit cold today. Maybe hell finally did freeze over. Now I'll have to keep all those promises I've made about "snowballs on a cold day in hell." Look out. The devil's turned off his burners. Satan's closed shop. Now he's come to collect.

The red devil man just came up and talked to me in his ski parka and asked me for a cigarette. So there is hope for hell. Tobacco, sin, the burning flame. I noticed that in addition to the red paint slathered all over his body, the devil also has dark black rings around his eyes, like tiny black pits of purgatory set in his face and he wears a brown felt fedora, pointy shoes and a black drawn-on moustache.

So he asks me for a cigarette and I say, "Okay, one cigarette coming up" but what I really mean is one going down down down, and I fish around in my bag and give him the smoke. The devil takes the cigarette, looks me in the eyes and says, "May you succeed in your every endeavor," and walks away. Exactly three minutes later he reappears, muttering, "Some people succeed at their every endeavor, but it's not necessarily a success," and he laughs and vanishes out of the world.

That devil is such a damn trickster. You can't take a wish from the devil and take it to heart. Doubt doubt doubt it and throw it over your left shoulder for the birds to feed on. The devil has a way about him, but throw that shit out yer door and kick it into the street. As much as you want to, as much as you long to believe - the devil is not your friend.

The red devil man is wearing a fluorescent-orange wind breaker today. Does he really think cars won't notice him without it on? He's painted tip to toe in red paint for godsake! I guess you can never be too careful. Best not to scrimp on safety-even in hell.

The red devil man is wearing a snappy grey wool blazer over his red outfit today. Guess he's feeling extra fancy tonight. Maybe he's going to dine on gourmet leftovers. For all I know, he's a wealthy insane millionaire who gets off on his self-purgatory devil-trip. Who knows? I watch him as he disappears into the gates of the hell that is the Mission.

I saw the red devil man again today outside of Muddy Waters. He was standing in the full glory of the day wearing a blue striped bathrobe. Seems like the devil man is really knocking himself out to make a statement this time. This bathrobe thing, it's like, "Satan, Reclined" or "Lucifer, Laid Back." A fashion triumph.

A friend told me today that the Devil guy was banned from the health food store he works at for brandishing a large sheath knife that he hides down his pants. Whoops. Guess I'll put a lid on my smart mouth around him next time. Getting taken out by Satan on a sidewalk in the

Mission has got to have some kind of apocalyptic karmic retribution. But then again, what a way to go.

Postal Rage

Standing in the post office line at Church and Market with my two small packages, some insane white dude walks in yelling to no one in particular, screams, "Bitch! You fucking ho! I'll put it up your ass, you ho. Put you in your place."

He came up and as chance will have it, stood right behind me. A little too close. His face was red as a lobster. "All you folks making a hundred thousand a year. You got your cars, got your money. And for what?"

The humble postal line - an old lady, a haggard housewife, a dude in a checkered shirt, a wrinkled Mexican man, and myself - all cringed forward trying not to look at him. We knew what he meant but it was all sorely misdirected towards us folks who shared his lower rung on the ladder of life. None of us really needed his shit on top of the truth. "Fucking ho bitch! I put a cap in yo ass!"

We were all silent as he stood screaming, leaning in towards me, his face turning redder and redder until I thought it might burst like a big rotten tomato. We were all silent as he insulted the world, insulted gays, women, and just about every other minority group imaginable.

All I had with me was my two packages and my little leopard handbag which was no contest to this man's fury. The next time I go to the post office I'm going to bring my mace. Maybe after a little pain we'll find out whose lobster-red ass runs outta there like a sorry little panty-waist. Life sucks. You gotta find a way to deal. Not on my time.

Crab

I was walking down Market Street near my house one day when I saw a fiddler crab sitting right in the middle of the sidewalk. I almost stepped on him by accident. I bent down wondering what the hell a little crab was doing sitting there in the middle of the city.

I bent down. "Hey there, little guy. What are you doing down there?"

No reply.

I nudged him with my foot and he sort of flopped around. I realized he was a rubber crab and reached down to pick him up. When I grabbed him he suddenly started wriggling around, waiving that big fiddler claw at me. He was real after all.

I pushed him carefully off to the side, out of the way of foot traffic and went home to get a cardboard box.

Ten minutes later I came back half expecting him to be lying there crushed in the sidewalk. Instead he was gone.

I looked all around and finally spotted him crawling sideways, his back against a building wall. Though he was only an inch and a half tall, he had his little claw weapons pointed upwards fending off his five-foot opponents.

After some crazy maneuvering and a fancy claw swordfight, I got him in the box and drove him out to the ocean. I dipped him in the water and dropped him off in the reeds where he probably baked to death or got eaten by a seagull or stepped on by some deadhead dropping acid. But anything's better then dying out on a San Francisco street where no one gives a shit about you and where you haven't got a chance in big city hell.

Good Head

Me and a friend were walking down Market Street when we came across some old decrepit beauty-school mannequin heads lolling around on the sidewalk like crash victims. A haggard brunette and blonde. We each took one and walked down the street, talking to our respective head.

We went to Bagdad Cafe with our heads for dates and sat down with the heads seated at their own places. People stared at us nonchalantly reading our menus.

One waiter came over and peered down at the blond in the seat next to me. "So are you gonna give me head later?" he laughed. It was a real kneeslapper, or would have been if they'd had knees to slap.

The wait staff liked them. They even brought our heads menus.

Gridlock

Driving through North Beach and Chinatown I got caught in a traffic block. For a mile in every direction there were cars. That's all there was. Stuck in my hot black car, slowly roasting on a rare scorching day in San Francisco, watching the lights turn green, yellow, red and back again without moving an inch, sweat-drenched, watching the day roll on by, my time wasted, wasted. Trying to find a hopeless parking space that I would never find from a dead end stoplight.

Looking for a parking space in San Francisco is like looking for God. You could run around for days and days and swear you'll never find it. Never find your little niche in the world. Then just when you've stopped looking, sure that it doesn't exist, you find one, a tiny space in the city. But you can barely fit inside. So you squeeze yourself in cockeyed, like you can interpret religion, desperate to fit *somewhere*, anywhere in the grand scheme of things.

Today in Chinatown there was no answer, no rationalization to be found. Slowly I rolled out of the tight jam and just went back home. I gave up in the struggle to find a parking space, in the struggle for life. Today I just didn't have it in me to fight.

Snaps

I was walking down the street with a friend and we were throwing those tiny "snaps" at each other. You know those little white exploding paper things? Well as we were walking down this sidewalk in Chinatown, an ancient Asian woman came out of her shop behind us and with a big toothless grin started stepping on the snaps that had fallen to the ground unexploded. We stopped and helped her stomp them all out while she laughed and laughed. What a cool lady.

Black Angel

One afternoon I saw a big blackbird in the street, standing statue still. While I watched, a car drove by and hit the bird. Drove right over it and I heard the crunch of its bones flattened on the pavement, its wings bent upward backward like a mangled black angel. The other crows swooped around and around, screeching at the still body.

The car never stopped. Just kept rolling by.

I just stood there and started to cry. Uncontrollably. Cried myself out of my body. I cried because it made no sense. I had forgotten how things were. I cried because the bird was sick and couldn't fly and the cars never, never stop. I should have known.

I cried because we all die, crushed under one wheel or another. I cried for the dead bird in the street. There was nothing I could do.

Spitting It Out

When I left my last boyfriend, something changed in me. Forever. It was powerful and beautiful like breaking open from a dark shell.

I suddenly decided. Just decided that I wasn't going to take any more bullshit from anyone. I wasn't going to let the opinions of others shape my life. I felt strong, powerful, sexy, free, happy. That pure happiness that comes from just being who you truly are, without apology to the world.

It suddenly became clear that I was not surrounded by like-minded people. As I changed, my life unfolded. I was doing the things I always dreamed of doing. Started a band, had a fucking great boyfriend. Started taking good care of myself, eating well and working out at the gym. Weekend drinking and having fun. Two of my best girlfriends just couldn't be happy for me. They were not happy themselves. I was surrounded by negative people in their own respective dark clouds because I had been so lost myself in the past. Instead of being happy for me and my strength, they acted threatened – jealous and weird. They couldn't accept who I had become. You've heard of fair weather friends - I had foul weather friends. They made snide remarks, thinly veiled insults and catty remarks about my appearance and my lifestyle. One friend was especially creepy, pointedly staring silently at my new boyfriend for disturbing lengths of time, just to fuck with me. Apparently she didn't have anything much better to do. At first I felt sorry for them. I thought it would change, but it went on and on. I tried talking it out to no avail. For a while I thought *what good is getting the things you want if everyone just resents you for it in the end?* Finally I just said *screw it* and left them behind too.

I took all those who had done me wrong and I burned them in my head like an effigy to the past. When I see them around town they don't exist to me. Just whorls of smoke like a distant memory, the past growing ever farther away from me.

My life was finally a clean slate. I would now be more guarded about who I let in close. In with the good, the creative, the unjudgmental - filtering out the duds.

I was going to be free, live my life how I wanted, make music, write, travel, be a sexy motherfucker. No going back. No apology. No apology for living my wild crazy way. My own way. No apology for being myself.

Ayn Imperato is a writer and musician. She is the author of *Greyhound to Wherever* (Andromeda Press), and her writing has appeared in *Maximum RocknRoll* and *Punk Planet*. This is her second collection of short stories. She lives in San Francisco.

Manic D Press Books

Please add $3.00 to all orders for postage and handling.

Manic D Press • Box 410804 • San Francisco CA 94141 USA

info@manicdpress.com   www.manicdpress.com

Distributed to the trade
in the US & Canada by Publishers Group West

in the UK & Europe by Turnaround Distribution